Tick, Tick, Boom!
Say U Promise 4

Tick, Tick, Boom!
Say U Promise 4

Ms. Michel Moore

www.urbanbooks.net

Urban Books, LLC
300 Farmingdale Road, NY-Route 109
Farmingdale, NY 11735

Tick, Tick, Boom! Say U Promise 4
Copyright © 2017 Ms. Michel Moore

ISBN 13: 978-1-62286-563-5
ISBN 10: 1-62286-563-4

First Trade Paperback Printing August 2017
Printed in the United States of America

10 9 8 7 6 5 4 3 2 1

This is a work of fiction. Any references or similarities to actual events, real people, living or dead, or to real locales are intended to give the novel a sense of reality. Any similarity in other names, characters, places, and incidents is entirely coincidental.

Distributed by Kensington Publishing Corp.
Submit orders to:
Customer Service
400 Hahn Road
Westminster, MD 21157-4627
Phone: 1-800-733-3000
Fax: 1-800-659-2436

Tick, Tick, Boom!
Say U Promise 4

by

Ms. Michel Moore

To my grandfather, James R. Sanders.
I miss you.

Acknowledgments

Thank God I'm of sound mind and body. Without Him, I'm nothing. He knows my heart. Special love to my family, friends, and the many readers who have rocked out with me since 2005. I appreciate each of you. Keep God first and know that the best is yet to come.

Chapter One

SAY IT AIN'T SO

"You backstabbing, conniving son of a crackhead. I can't believe you think it's gonna be all good. Hell to the naw. That treating me like my feelings don't matter bullshit is definitely over. Matter of fact, so is me and you. You and that illegitimate bastard you care so damn much about can have each other. I'm done with all this bullshit. Fuck you and my sister. Y'all can have each other. Be one big happy-go-lucky family."

"Hold tight, girl. Are you serious and shit?"

"You think I'm not when I am? You got me all the way twisted." Kenya seethed with undeniable anger with the situation she had been forced to be a part of for months on end.

"So okay, bae, it's like that, is it?"

Kenya had no delay in her swift response. She meant every single word that rolled off her quivering lips. "Look, kick rocks, Storm. Trust it's just fucking like that!"

What the entire fuck? Just who in the hell do Kenya think she's talking to like that? She out of her rabbit-ass mind. She must be high. I made that crazy bird a boss bitch. I put her ass on top in this city and now she talking that garbage out the side of her mouth. After all the expensive, lavish gifts he'd showered her with, the numerous times he'd forgiven her complicated lies, and all the confusion she'd brought into his life, now he was pissed. Storm couldn't believe his ears and the slick-mouthed way his fiancée had just spoken to him before hanging up in his face.

That dumb bitch gonna spit all that venom on my unborn seed like that. I'm a grown-ass man. Flat out, I do what I wanna do for mines. Telling me to come get my clothes and get the hell outta my own damn crib like she paying bills. That Detroit-born mentality, strong-arm bullshit she be on got me all the way fucked up. Enough is enough. I swear to God when I get back home it's on. Kenya can't stop or slow down shit I got popping. I been making that gangsta noise since the womb. I should've known better. She ain't shit but a headache waiting to damn happen.

In the middle of his mental rant, he was snapped out of his thoughts. A strange car slowly pulling up on the other side of the abandoned factory warehouse now had his full attention. Kenya's fiery attitude, emotions, and demands would have to be put on hold. He had real business on the floor. Storm focused on the vehicle and its every movement.

Glancing at his watch, he took notice that it was seven o'clock on the nose. He was definitely on time for the meeting just like he'd promised Brother Rasul he would be. *Well, here the fuck we go. This is it. A nigga straight about to get that real plug on that real shit.* Rubbing his sweaty palms together, his mind raced on the possibilities these soon-to-be uncut drugs he was copping would bring to him and his struggling crew. The corners, spots, and territory that he and his brother had fought for over the years would be untouchable. They would become legendary kingpins who would be talked about for years to come. Storm took a deep breath.

He waited anxiously for the driver to make the first move in contacting him. With his cell phone now in hand, he didn't blink. He didn't move, but his eyes stayed watchful. This was a chance of a lifetime for him to really come back up in the game and get back on his feet. Reminiscing on all the bad luck he'd suffered over the past year, mostly thanks to Kenya and London, he didn't want to mess things up by overplaying his position.

Seconds later, the midnight black Dodge Challenger started to creep. Cautiously it approached Storm's general direction. As his heartbeat pounded with eager anticipation, not fear, he tossed his phone over onto the passenger seat. Unarmed, as he was instructed to be, he felt slightly naked, but it was what it was. He understood he had to earn trust. Yet, instinctively from growing up in the streets, Storm kept his foot on the brake while the car was still in drive, just in case this was some sort of setup bullshit. Dealing in the line of work he did, anything could and would happen at a drop of a dime. If there was one thing Storm knew for sure, it was that hustlers definitely had no honor among thieves. Just because his woman's homeboy, Brother Rasul, had hooked him up with this meeting, that meant nothing. After the way Kenya had just spoken to him, everything seemed suspicious.

Raising his left hand to shield the last bit of shine from the setting sun, Storm tightened up his right grip on the steering wheel. The vehicles, now side by side, both revved their engines as if they were preparing to race. When the driver of the Challenger finally lowered the tinted window the anticipation of what to expect was ended. Storm was more than relieved, as well as shocked, to see a female posted up behind the wheel.

"Hey, what up, doe." The platinum blonde beauty grinned, winking her eye. "Park your whip, baby boy, and come take a ride with me!"

Hearing the chick say, "What up, doe," Storm immediately recognized she must've been from Detroit. *Oh, hell naw. Not another one of these females. What in the entire fuck?* "Yeah, okay, but hold tight. Where we going?" his first mind told him to ask before stepping out his car.

"To the beach, out to dinner, and then maybe to the show," she teased sarcastically before cutting to the chase. "Look, guy, are you riding or not? Because if you want me to go back and say you told me to get the fuck on and you wasn't interested in getting in the car with my cute ass, I can do that too. Shit, it ain't a problem. I'ma get paid regardless any way it go. So that's on you. The choice is yours."

Trusting that Brother Rasul wouldn't send him on a dummy mission, especially knowing it would hurt Kenya in the long run, Storm put his car in park. Turning off the ignition he smoked the female over after getting out of his vehicle. "Damn, girl, slow ya roll. I'm coming!"

Clicking the automatic locks, the feisty, sharp-tongued driver allowed Storm to get inside and shut the door. "Look, man, I hope you ain't got no guns or bullshit like that on you. Because if you do—"

"Naw, my dude already told me ahead of time. I'm straight." Paranoid, he looked in the back seat to make sure no one was hiding there on a sneak ambush attack mission. "Okay, so now what's next? Where we headed and why can't I just follow you?"

"Damn, boy, you ask way too many questions. You sure you ain't the police?"

"Say what?" Storm frowned at even the implication of being a so-called officer of the law.

"Look, nigga, just sit back, relax, and ride. That's what's next." Respecting his gangsta for checking out his surroundings, she sized him up while running her fingers through her braids. "You wanna win or what?" the girl asked, laughing after blowing a nice-sized bubble with the gum she was chewing. Mysteriously, the female then sent a text to someone, before pulling off.

Just then Storm realized that not only was he at a total disadvantage not having a gun to at least have a fighting chance to protect himself if any wild shit jumped off, but he'd left his cell phone back in his car as well. "Hey, hold up. I need my phone," he abruptly blurted out.

"Look, guy, didn't I say just sit back and ride?" She shook her head and smirked before turning out of the deserted parking lot. "I see you one of them damn hard-headed recruits. I already done texted that we was on our way, so we on the clock with it and I ain't being late for no-damn-body, not even Jesus."

Having a flashback to the tropical island and all the torture Javier put him through while he was being held hostage, Storm manned up, rubbing his ear, which was missing the lobe courtesy of his past host. Just thinking about the entire ordeal made him get a headache. It seemed like it was only yesterday. Sadly his mind drifted back.

After carefully observing Storm's and Deacon's response to seeing the picture, he then reacted. He waved his hand and had his men remove both Storm and Deacon to a back room. Storm was totally speechless and in shock. He couldn't understand what he had just seen.

Deacon was terrified. "Damn, man, what the fuck is Kenya off into? I knew that bitch was to fucking good to be true. I can't believe this shit! What did she say she was flying out East for anyway?" He asked Storm question after question.

"Listen, Deacon, I swear to you, guy, I don't know what the fuck is going on. Maybe these old cats are trying to test us or something? Besides, it was your boy Zack who turned us on to her in the first place. So stop pointing fucking fingers."

They were confused as hell and scared of what the outcome might be. The two friends paced the floor as they tried to think of an explanation for the shit they were in. After about an hour or so of being locked in the room, they heard footsteps approaching. They both started to sweat as they watched the doorknob start to turn. The door was swung wide open, and a group of men rushed in, followed by Javier. He entered the room and focused all of his attention on Storm. He had the picture of Kenya and Storm dangling from his hand. Javier had his men search Storm's luggage, and they found the picture along with a piece of paper in his wallet.

"You men have your orders." Javier gave his crew a slight nod. Some of his men grabbed Deacon by his throat dragging him out of the room. He was begging for his life as he struggled to breathe. His eyes were bulging out of his head. "Don't beg! It shows no pride. Be a man," was all that Javier said in a nonchalant manner, while still watching Storm. Deacon didn't take Javier's advice and could be heard screaming as they took him in the basement. Javier seemed cold and unbothered about what was obviously about to take place. Deacon was on his way to hell.

"Please, Javier! I don't know what's going on. I swear to God!" Storm was panicking. "I know it looks bad, but listen: that girl on the picture can't be my girl. It doesn't make sense. My woman is down for me. She loves me!"

Javier's men threw Storm in a chair and tied him up. He was still trying to explain, even though he didn't understand himself. Even though he was facing death, he couldn't understand how his beloved Kenya could betray him. "It's not her! It must be a mistake! Let me call her! She can explain!"

"*Please don't play with my intelligence. The way you looked at that picture was a dead giveaway of your guilt and if I wanted more proof, you yourself provided it to me. So please stop with the lies.*" Javier held the picture of Storm and Kenya up next to the picture that he'd passed around earlier. He asked Storm once again, "*Do you care to try to explain?*" Storm just shook his head and looked toward the ground. "*I didn't think so,*" Javier mocked.

Storm was in shock. The girl in the picture looked just like Kenya, only without makeup. How could this be? Storm was lost in his thoughts. How could this be his Kenya; but how could it not be? The final nail in the coffin came as Javier held up the paper that he had gotten out of Storm's wallet. He read the words that headlined the page: MOTOWN STORAGE UNITS. It was the same receipt that Storm found in the closet and wanted to ask Kenya about.

Javier read off the name that was at the bottom of the page. Storm heard the name and couldn't believe what he heard. His mouth dropped open.

"*I guess that you still don't know who London Roberts is, do you?*"

Storm was heartbroken. Not because he knew he was about to die, but because he believed that Kenya had betrayed him.

Javier motioned for his men to take Storm away. They untied Storm and snatched him up from the chair. Unlike Deacon, he didn't scream, as he was led away to the unknown. Javier and his men couldn't hurt him any worse than he believed that his cherished Kenya had already done.

He came back to the present. *Oh, well, it ain't no retirement plan to this game. When you in, you all the way in. You hustle, grind, get pussy, then fucking die.*

For now, Storm's mindset was focused on staying alive and securing the new plug. It wasn't on London and his soon-to-be-born son, not on Marco and his murderous threats, and not on Kenya's temper tantrums and pity parties she'd recently become famous for throwing. He'd deal with her and all that other chaotic madness later; that was, if he made it back alive in one piece.

O.T. ran through countless red lights. He disobeyed every law on the books in pursuit of getting to a very much distressed London as soon as possible. On a mission, he smashed the accelerator damn near to the floor of his car. Relentlessly pushing redial on his cell phone, he attempted to reach London or at least Kenya. In panic mode, he received nothing but a busy signal. From the drastic tone in London's voice, O.T. realized that this wasn't a false alarm or no fucking practice run. This shit was real, and it must truly be time for her to deliver his nephew, the baby he wished was his seed.

He didn't know what had changed him or his selfish way of thinking over the past few months. Whatever it was he knew he had to be there for London and the baby. Driving down the final stretch of road before turning into his brother's semi-gated community, O.T. got a glimpse of a car. Looking up into the rearview mirror it was more than obvious that the car seemed to be following him. Yet, considering what he believed was going on at the condo, he couldn't care less about the ho-ass police stopping him for violating a couple of traffic laws. His normal mindset was *fuck the police,* and today was no different. After all the different times cops in his city had been caught on tape violating people's rights, O.T. didn't care. As far as he was concerned, they could provide him and London with a special VIP police escort to the hospital if they wanted to.

Turning onto the block, O.T. had to slow his car down. He had to avoid colliding with the massive convoy of Mexican workers, huge trailers, lawn mowers, blowers, and Dumpsters that lined the road. Cautiously driving over the speed bumps in an attempt not to bend his rims, he was finally near Storm's condo.

Shit, thank fucking God I'm here. I swear I hope London is good. I hope she and my little nephew are both a hundred. That last thing she needs is all that extra stress she been going through with my damn brother and Kenya's wild attitude-having ass.

Having no choice but to park several doors down, O.T. swerved over near the curb. Wanting nothing more than to be London's hood Prince Charming, he turned off the engine and reached for his cell. Jumping out of his ride, which was packed with bags containing stuff for the baby, O.T. shut the door with a smirk on his face. Ignoring the fact that the car he felt was following him had also made its way down the heavily populated block, he kept it moving. In good spirits, the seasoned thug started jogging over toward the condo knowing he was only yards away from seeing London.

"Hey, nigga. What's up, you coward slimeball motherfucker?" The hooded driver of the other car then also swerved up near the curb, getting out with gun in hand. Wasting no time, the pistol was raised, and the intent was apparent.

O.T. froze. He was almost speechless. He was shocked this field Negro was so brazen to come where he laid his head. Not to mention trying to get ignorant and then be ballsy enough to point a gun at him. O.T. felt his blood pressure jump and his anger intensify. He wasn't scared to have a gun pointed at him. He was born into the street life, and he was definitely accustomed to gunplay. Instinctively, he stood like a solider ready to go to war before he spoke. His tone was filled with utter disdain and not a single inch of fear. "Oh, yeah? Damn, I must be seeing things. Have you lost your fucking mind? I ought to—"

"Ought to what? You ought to what, ho-ass nigga? Shut the entire fuck up and be a man?"

Instead of being terrified, O.T. was amused. He laughed as he responded to the unexpected interruption to his day. "Come the hell on. Get yourself out that fantasy you and your crew be so deep off into. What in the fuck do you know about being a damn man? Matter of fact, get the fuck on, bitch. I got business to take care of inside and I ain't got time for this little gangsta moment you having!"

"You and ya fake-ass brother think y'all can go around ruining people lives, huh? You and him thinking it ain't no consequences to that bullshit y'all do, but trust when I tell you it fucking is. And you gonna pay; today."

"Listen, you twisted-hearted piece of garbage," O.T. bossed up boldly shouting loud enough for the Mexicans working on the block to hear. "If I'm supposed to be scared because you got a little gun, then you dead-ass wrong this go-around. The way my bloodline is set up, being a sucker is impossible. Now if you gonna do something, then strap on your nuts, pretend you man enough to do it, or beat it, you feel me? But just know I'm gonna hunt ya black ass down until the day I die for coming out here to my brother's crib like you some gangsta on a mission."

"Oh, yeah, you real tough right about now while I'm holding this gun. Who in the hell you think you is, some ghetto, nappy-headed Superman or something, like you can't bleed blood?"

"Fuck you with ya bitch ass. I guess you officially ain't man enough, huh?" O.T. spat on the front grass before turning around to head for the condo's front door.

Hearing him making threats, acting as if he were untouchable and above getting got, the hooded driver easily pulled the trigger. Once, twice, three times, then four. Each one seemed louder than the last. The thunderous echo of a total of eight loud gunshots filled the air. As each silver-colored shell casing hit the concrete, sheer pandemonium ensued. Quickly taking cover behind trucks, trees, bushes, and garbage cans, innocent bystanders were forced to bear witness to what could only be described as tragic. O.T.'s body jerked, absorbing bullet after bullet before hitting the ground. Seconds later the hooded shooter jumped back in the car and recklessly sped off.

As the stunned spectators emerged from the safety of whatever they'd found to seek refuge with, getting out of harm's way, they couldn't believe their eyes. The driver of the first car that came barreling down the block only minutes earlier was sprawled out in a flower-lined driveway. It was more than easy to see he had bullet holes seemingly everywhere on his body. With clots of blood trickling from the corner of his lips, his condition was definitely dire. This type of thing never happened in this exclusive gated community, so many were terrified, stunned, and speechless.

Gaining courage after making sure the shooter was long gone, some of the bolder neighbors who were now in their own front yards cautiously approached O.T. With their cordless phones in hand, some called 911 begging for an ambulance and, of course, the police. O.T. was potentially bleeding out, struggling to breathe.

The elderly homeowner of the driveway, old Mrs. Farrow, went to knock on Storm and Kenya's door. She knew that if they were home, despite the sounds of a radio playing through the door, they'd certainly have heard the loud barrage of gunfire. It'd interrupted their otherwise quiet community. The elderly neighbor opted to knock just the same. Recognizing O.T. as one of their frequent visitors, she felt it was the right thing to do.

She pounded her clenched fist several times then waited. Mrs. Farrow repeated the act a few more times. Getting no answer, the woman, known as the neighborhood busybody, rejoined the others. Trying to make the young man as comfortable as possible while they waited for the ambulance, they all relived the surprise misfortune. Thankfully, minutes later, help arrived. O.T., fighting to live so he could help London raise his brother's baby, was rushed to the nearest hospital.

"We losing him. Shit, we losing him. Damn, hurry," the EMT panicked as the gauge on the heart monitor wildly beeped, signaling time was crucial. "Fuck, fuck, fuck, he's about to go into shock. He's lost so much blood, and his vitals are crazy." Coming to the realization that life was rapidly fading away from the victim of multiple bullet wounds he was treating, the trained technician faced the cold, hard facts. Limited in what procedures he could perform in transit, the man nervously checked his watch. "If we don't get him stabilized in the next two to three minutes, this boy is as good as dead. These gaping holes need dealing with now! He's choking on his own fluids. Hurry!"

"I know. I hear the machines back there going berserk. I radioed ahead for a team to be waiting because we need top priority as soon as we pull in." With his partner trying everything to save the young man's life, the ambulance driver ran through the red lights with sirens blaring. Listening to the agonizing sounds of the wounded victim gagging, he pressed the gas pedal to the floor. With the hospital finally in sight, he roared into the emergency room entrance with a prayer in his heart.

Surrounded by doctors as well as a police detective, the grim reality set in about what the outcome would be. It was beyond hard to be positive as O.T.'s motionless, bullet-riddled body was removed from the rig. Strapped to a gurney, face pale as a ghost, he was rushed into the triage area. His bloodied clothes were cut off and tossed into clear plastic bags. Along with the combination of several needles roughly stuck in his skin, IV bags were hung to the side. Barely finding a heartbeat, they immediately pressed an oxygen mask on his face. O.T., a certified hood warrior, remained unconscious, not making a sound.

"Okay, what do we have?" The senior trauma surgeon on staff entered the chaotic room. He hoped for the best but expected the worst. "What's the initial damage and what are his vitals? Everyone please don't speak at once."

"Doctor, from what we can tell, he has suffered five gunshot wounds in total. Three seem to have gone in and out through his lower extremities. Thank God those three don't seem to be life-threatening. Yet, since the patient has yet to speak, the possibility of spinal damage is still very much possible," Head Trauma Nurse Jamison, who had seen it all throughout the years, gravely reported from her first evaluation. "However, the other two bullets appear to have struck major organs, one possibly ripping right through his kidney. From what the first responders tell me was the amount of blood on the scene, along with the massive amounts lost while he was being transported, I'm more than extremely concerned. His breathing is almost nonexistent. His pressure is also low."

Putting white rubber gloves on, Dr. Wang sternly ordered all unnecessary persons immediately outside of the triage examination room. As if on cue, O.T. went into violent convulsions. His arms wildly flung while his muscle-chiseled chest heaved upward and down at a rapid pace.

"Remember, Doc, if he says anything I need to know, and any slugs you might be lucky enough to recover—"

"Listen, Officer whatever your name is, I'm trying to save this man's life. Anything else is secondary to me. Now, like I just told everyone else, leave and let me do my job." Dr. Wang angrily turned his back on the unsympathetic cop. His first priority was to focus on his patient, who was officially identified by the pushy policeman as twenty-three-year-old Othello Terrence Christian, a target of several criminal investigations throughout the years.

When the double steel doors of the emergency room swung shut, the officer took out his cell phone, calling his superior. "Hey, Malloy, it's me. Yeah, man, they have that cocky motherfucker in the back right now working on him. But, from the looks of things to me, if that fool makes it to see the sunrise it's gonna be nothing short of a goddamn miracle. It looks like that dyke done turned him into Swiss cheese and is about to send him to meet his Maker. Remind me not to send flowers to that bitch boy's funeral or contribute to any fundraisers!"

Chief Detective Malloy shut his cell, sliding it back on the clip on his side. Looking at his partner, he smiled delivering the encouraging update. "Oh, well, with that deranged lunatic Marco Meriwether finally in custody and one of the Christian brothers out of our hair, things are looking up on closing a lot of open cases. Now if we can·put Storm out of commission, too, we'll be batting a thousand."

"Don't worry; he's the next domino to fall in this game for sure. The surveillance team might have lost him for the time being, but bet five dollars to a bucket of shit, he'll surface, especially since his brother is kicking down the devil's door!"

Having just arrived on the first of two very much still-active crime scenes, Malloy and Sergeant Kendricks got out of their unmarked vehicle. Raising the yellow tape, they approached the crashed rental Tangelina Marie Gibson had taken her final breath inside of after opening fire on O.T. A beige canvas tarp covered the body of the deceased as a small crowd of bystanders gathered on the still-damp street.

"Okay, Officer. What exactly went down?" Malloy questioned, watching the water department finish sealing the hole where the fire hydrant once stood before getting barreled over.

"Well, Detective, I was posted just like I was ordered to do."

"And?"

"And I thought it was Marco. It looked just like him. He—I mean, she—fit the description." The rookie undercover officer paced near Tangy's dead body, which housed a police-issued slug right between the eyes. "The hood, the braids, damn, damn, damn!"

"Listen, calm down and get back to the story." Malloy tried to keep him focused on the details and only the details. "What went down exactly blow by blow?"

Lighting a Marlboro cigarette to subdue his shaky nerves, he continued. "First she jumped out the car and ran up on him. They exchanged words; then she just opened fire on him, maybe seven or eight shots. I'm not sure!" His white, pale hands shook while taking a couple of pulls from his cigarette. "Then right after I told you to send backup, things really went berserk. The girl jumped back in the car! She just kept coming! She wouldn't stop!"

The officer had tossed the two-way radio on the passenger's seat before posting up. Knocking over several garbage cans and hitting a car in an attempt to get away from the homicide that was just committed, the driver was faced with the undercover officer's gun pointed directly at the windshield. "Stop or I'll fucking shoot!" he'd said.

Not paying attention to the officer's threats, the car had barreled through the one-man barricade, leaving no other recourse but more gunshots to ensue. Losing control of the automobile after being fatally struck by one of the bullets, the driver had crashed into a fire hydrant and slumped over to the side of the passenger seat. As the cocky but nervous policeman, with his pistol still drawn, approached the vehicle through the heavy water flow spewing from the hydrant, he had cautiously opened the door, snatching the hood off the driver. As all the braids fell out of the hood, he got a good look at the deceased's face.

"I couldn't believe it. A woman! I shot a goddamn woman!" He sat down as gawkers whispered, taking photos and videos with their cell phones.

"Look, man, it was you or her from what you just said. It can't be no holiday every day in our job. Death comes with the territory." Malloy placed his hand on the officer's shoulder. "And every cop's main objective is to go home at night to their families. You didn't kill the carpet-munching dyke." He glanced over at the now bloodstained tarp. "She had a death wish and killed her-damn-self!"

After getting the full rundown of the events leading up to the shooting and crash, the mood still seemed solemn. Even though Tangy thought she was every bit a man, she was still a female: a once-a-month-bleeding, emotional, unstable, jealous-hearted female. The fact that she appeared to attempt a premeditated murder and elude arrest offered no relief of guilt for the young Caucasian officer who was forced to take her obviously troubled life. With his face buried in his hands, Kendricks consolingly sat on the curb next to him.

On to investigate the most important crime scene, Malloy made his way down the road. Walking toward the front yard of the condo belonging to Storm, he instantly grew angry at what he'd just heard. *That crazy-ass girl robbed me of seeing the look on O.T.'s face when we arrested him and his older brother on conspiracy, racketeering, drug trafficking, and murder charges. I know I should be thanking her, but fuck; I had hours tied up in these damn cases!*

Observing his fellow officers conduct interviews with the Mexican landscaping crew who were witness to the shooting along with a few neighbors, Malloy stood near a trail of blood droplets on the concrete. With ten to twelve small cones marking important evidence to be collected, he was careful not to contaminate the area. Peering over at Storm's undoubtedly high-priced condo, he wanted nothing more than to have his men kick the door in and search the premises for any weapons or drugs. However, for the time being, he couldn't prove Storm, aka Tony Christian, had broken any laws, so the presumed empty dwelling was off-limits.

"Okay, you guys. Check everything out with a fine-toothed comb; then let's all meet back at the station. It ain't no use in watching this location anymore. We'll pick up the tail on Storm as soon as he shows up at the hospital to see about his brother." Making sure a thorough investigation took place before he and his officers finally packed up leaving the crime scene, Malloy took one last good look at Storm's condo. *One day I'm gonna get that warrant,* he promised himself, thinking he saw the closed drapes slightly move as he drove off. *One damn day.*

Slipping in and out of consciousness from losing so much blood, London was barely aware of what was going on. Now Kenya, the same person she'd deliberately taunted less than an hour ago, leaned down over her with the knife in her hands, lifting the newborn up. Taking the bread twists, she wrapped them tightly around the blood-filled umbilical cord and deviously smiled as she thought about Storm. Then vindictively glaring at her reflection in the shiny sides of the butcher knife, she cut it off, severing all ties the baby had with London.

"Where you going with my baby?" a weak and drained London muttered as the gunshot wound continued to bleed. "Let me hold him. Let me hold my baby," she begged as she started gagging on her own blood.

"Your baby?" Kenya questioned, wrapping the crying infant in the dish towels. Dazed, she sat down in Storm's favorite chair, rocking him in her arms as she watched her sister struggle to hold on to life. "You must have made a mistake. This is my baby, mine and Storm's!"

"But we're family. We're all we got. I love you, Kenya, please." London sadly took her last breath.

"Say u promise," Kenya nonchalantly replied. She smirked, looking down toward the floor and ignoring the fact her twin sister had just died in front of her eyes because she opted not to get her any help. Those three little words might have seemed like nothing to most people, but for the twins, they meant the world. It was their bond. Their way of letting each other know they had the other's back; no questions asked.

But now it was different. Kenya felt London had crossed the line between them months ago when having sex with Storm. Whether or not Kenya believed the twisted tale her twin and supposed man told about the way the betrayal went down, Kenya couldn't care less. Her sister chose to carry her man's seed, so it was what it was and had been for months: war.

Fast-forward to now. Kenya had officially lost it. She was full-blown deranged. There would be no turning back the hands of time. The pair of them could not sit on the steps of Gran's house daydreaming about places they wanted to travel to. There would be no more sharing of ice cream cones. No more running up and down the block chasing behind the other or brushing of hair before bedtime. Their biological twin magic powers were dead. When London took her last breath and left the land of the living, Kenya's spirit and soul were deceased but had yet to realize it.

Turning the volume of the music up in an attempt to ignore the sounds of the frantic neighbor's knocks who'd recognized O.T. as the gunshot victim, Kenya, who had obviously lost her mind, hummed to her now deceased twin sister's newborn son while she patiently waited for his daddy to return home so they could be one big, happy family. "Don't worry, li'l one, your real mommy's here with you."

Callously allowing her twin sister to die right before her eyes on the living room floor, Kenya seemed coldly unaware of what she'd truly just done. She rocked back and forth with London's defenseless newborn tucked in her arms, and the knocks at the front door soon stopped. As the smooth sounds of jazz flowed throughout the room, Kenya cried staring down at her nephew, Storm's son. *Despite what anybody says, you belong to me! I deserved to have had you, not that man-stealing bitch over there!* She nodded toward London. *Storm loves me! Not her, me! Even though I can't have no babies, he loves me!* Taking her still blood-covered hands Kenya used her fingertips to trace the tiny outline of the baby's lips. "Look at you," she softly spoke to him. "You got those big brown eyes just like my Gran used to have. And look at all that wavy hair."

The last track on the CD finally played. When the music stopped, Kenya kinda snapped out of her strange, oblivious trance, squinting her eyes. Seeing her twin sister with a bullet hole in her shoulder and a messy combination of blood and afterbirth spilled out between her still-open legs, it hit her like a ton of bricks. Quickly leaping up, Kenya laid the infant still wrapped in dishrags down on the couch, and she peeped back out the window. *Damn, who in the hell got hurt?* She quickly closed the drapes after seeing the crowd of people move out of the way so an ambulance could get through. *But who gives a sweet fuck? I got my own bullshit to deal with right now.*

Interrupting her selfish thoughts of *me, me, me,* Storm's son started to wiggle on the couch. Momentarily thinking clearly for the first time since smacking the dog shit out of London, Kenya knew she had to get the infant some much-needed medical attention. Leaning over London's still body, Kenya broke all the way down as she checked for a pulse. "Oh my God! What did I just fucking do? I'm sorry! I'm sorry!" she sobbed, holding London's limp hand and knowing a piece of herself would forever be missing. Apologizing in one breath while still going hard in the next, Kenya trembled as she spoke. "I didn't mean it! I promise I didn't! But why did you have to keep that baby? Why? Why? You knew that shit was foul! You know he didn't rape you!"

Of course, there was no movement from her twin sister. No acceptance of Kenya's erratic excuses or begging to hold her newborn. No whining about having to abruptly drop out of school and, lastly, much to Kenya's delight, no calling out for Storm. Letting her grip of London's hand go, Kenya glanced over her shoulder at the now whimpering infant.

You. You fucking little bastard! Spitefully, with her hair practically standing on top of her head, she focused her attention to the small bundle of otherwise joy who was the painful source of all her problems. *You, the one who made my sister stab me in the back and made Storm act a fool. A trust fund for your punk ass, a life insurance policy, for real? All that for you? After I been riding with that nigga and all his gangsta bullshit! Oh, hell naw!*

Coldly staring at the innocent baby, blaming him for the troubles of the world he was just born into, Kenya was soon distracted. Out of the corner of her eye, she saw the shiny, jagged edges of the blood-covered butcher knife used to cut the umbilical cord. Still on the floor, she crawled around London's body snatching the wooden handle up and clutching it tightly in her hand. With the blade facing the baby, Kenya continued her rant. "Why did you have to be a boy? Why? I wanted Storm's first-born and you robbed me of that," she mumbled standing to her feet. Slowly walking toward her tiny nephew and stepson to be, Kenya once again totally zoned out. "If it weren't for you, life would've still been perfect around this bitch. But you fucked that up for me, didn't you?"

With each step, the once self-proclaimed Detroit boss bitch diva became more and more out of touch with reality. Finally standing over the naked, wide-eyed baby, Kenya let the pointed tip of the knife she normally used to cut chicken and beef press down on his birthmark, which was located exactly where Storm's was. *I should just slit your damn throat, you little troublemaker! You straight foul!* Noticing again his brown eyes looked like her beloved Gran's, Kenya felt chill bumps race down her arms. *I just wanna be happy.* She cried. *I want things back the way they were for me and Storm.*

Letting revenge win over family loyalty, Kenya still had no remorse in her heart for what she allowed to just happen to London and worse than that what she was about to do to London's newborn: Storm's illegitimate seed.

Chapter Two

"So, damn, I guess you're from Detroit, huh?" Storm tried making idle conversation as he continued to pay attention to the direction they were headed in.

"What?" She slightly eased up on the gas pedal as the traffic flow increased.

"Detroit. I said, you from Detroit?" Storm continued to make mental notes about every twist, turn, and lane change they were making. In his mind, it would be better to be safe than sorry just in case he had to bail out of the moving car and attempt to make it back to the city on foot. Yeah, he may have had to suffer a broken bone or two, but at least he'd be alive.

"And? So, big deal. What if I am?"

"Damn, ma, why you so coldblooded? I was just asking a question, making idle conversation. My girl is from there. She say that 'what up, doe' shit too. So damn slow pump the attitude."

"Well, okay, good for her Detroit-born ass." She whipped the Challenger down on the freeway heading out of the city limits. "You want a cookie or some gay shit like that 'cause you fucking a bitch from the D? Probably some cum Dumpster bird who swing from a pole in that ratchet club you was running?"

If it'd been any other day or any other female, all hell would have broken out. Storm would've chin-checked her by now for that smart-ass hood rat attitude and running off at the mouth. He felt his heart rate increase and his adrenalin pump. Forget the fact that she could have been driving him to his death, the hardcore drug dealer wanted to smack some manners into her. He was a man and demanded respect from whoever, whenever. He wanted nothing more than to clown, but since she was obviously his gateway to the connect, he chilled. "You know what, I'ma take your advice and just sit back until we get where we going 'cause you straight bugging. And if a nigga like me feed off into your smart mouth, shit gonna go to the left real quick."

Never taking her eyes off the road, the no-nonsense female blew another bubble. With a snarl on her face, she rolled her eyes popping the gum with her long fingernails. "Okay, see yeah, that's what in the fuck I'm talking about. Good, 'cause see a bitch like me, I hate questions, and I hate motherfuckers who ask them even more. See to me that's some type of police bullshit. That's where the fuck I'm at with mines!"

Forty minutes or so of riding finally came to a conclusion. With an obvious disdain for her passenger, the box-braided, sassy-mouthed driver pulled into the parking lot of an off-brand one-story motel. From the looks of the cars there, it was apparent to Storm this spot was far from the five-star establishments he was accustomed to staying in.

Finding a spot not to close to the other vehicles, she checked her rearview mirror. After killing the engine, she then stretched her arms upward and yawned. Leaning over damn near in Storm's lap, she opened the glove compartment. Glancing up at him she smirked while removing a key before getting out the car. Following her lead, Storm got out the car as well carefully observing what and who were in his close proximity. As the girl headed to the building's last room with an outside door entrance, Storm stayed close behind.

"Look, damn, girl, how much longer this silly-ass bullshit cat-and-mouse game gonna go down? I mean, we been at this for damn near an entire hour. Now is we gonna see the so-called man? Or even the man's man for that matter?"

"Damn, nigga, here the fuck you go with the freaking questions again! Stop having all these weak-minded gangster moments. I'm not freaking amused." Sticking the key in the door, she slipped inside the dark room immediately hitting the light switch. "Well, are you coming in or what?" She sucked her teeth looking back at Storm who was more than hesitant to step through the threshold.

"Dig this, I ain't sign up for all this espionage, secret squirrel games you playing!" He looked over his shoulder and scanned the parking lot for any activity looking out of the way. "Enough is fucking enough! I'm done!"

Storm's tirade and wannabe boss demeanor had finally broken through the girl's otherwise tough exterior. Liking his general overall swag, she decided to give him a low-key heads-up; he was closer than he thought to become a major force in the Dallas drug trade. "Listen, dude, come on inside and get ready okay? I need to make this shit happen so I can hurry up and get home to my man! You doing too much right about now; fuck. Damn just stop acting straight pussy. If I was gonna kill your pretty ass don't you think you'd be dead by now?"

Reading in between the lines, cautiously Storm entered the room. Shutting the door behind him, he bossed all the way up. "Okay, big shit talker, I'm inside, so now what? What's really good?" Before he could say another word, his beautiful-complexioned escort shocked him by taking off her shirt. As her full C-cup breasts practically spilled out of her lace bra, Storm stood mute and confused. Seconds later, she unzipped her shorts wiggling out of them. When they hit the floor, being a man, Storm's dick started to get hard. Seeing countless dancers at Alley Cats night after night had numbed him to the typical freak shit, but this was a strange, unexpected pleasure. "Damn, ma, it's like that? What kinda freak shit you about to get off into? You got a brother straight confused."

"Nigga, please, so you checking for me huh? That's cute as a motherfucker." She smiled reaching behind her back and unfastening her bra. "But please don't play yourself! You fine and all, but I'm here chasing money, that almighty dollar, not dick! Now if you was Benjamin Franklin, then you'd be on. I'd be on my knees by now sucking you off like it was no tomorrow. But unfortunately, you ain't. You just some hood nigga from around the way waiting to get blessed by the hustle gods!" Finally naked and done going on about Storm's ill-placed thought process, she walked over to the dresser. Grabbing a swimming suit and a pair of trunks she was almost ready. Grinning with satisfaction, she tossed Storm the navy blue trunks. "Okay, playboy." She swooped her braids up in a ponytail teasing him with her body she knew he lusted after. "Your turn. Drop them jeans and put these on."

"What?" he said, puzzled, taking a few steps backward and wondering where all this was going.

"Come on, guy. We got a date poolside, so chop chop! Hurry the hell up. I already done told you I'm on the clock."

"The sun almost damn down, so what the hell we going to the pool for? And what in the hell a guy need to put these shits on for? I'm straight on all that extra you here trying to push on me."

"Damn here the fuck we go with all the police, badge, and gun questions again." She shook her head. "Just hurry up and come the hell on. You wasting time."

Even though Storm was pissed with his girl, he was still loyal to Kenya, but the sheer thought of hitting some strange pussy, especially some as sexy as the pussy was in front of him, was overwhelming. Knowing full well he was about to meet the connect, he still couldn't help the fact his dick was now rock hard. Doing as instructed, Storm stripped down showing his perfectly chiseled body. Watching the sassy-talking female lick her lips, and the sight of her long braids practically touching the crack of her ass when she turned around, Storm wanted nothing more than to bang her lights out. However, that would have to wait, hopefully for another date and another time.

Finally dressed in their swim attire, they grabbed towels and headed for the pool located in the rear of the cheap motel. When they got poolside, she immediately told Storm to see if the water was cold as she sat down in the semi-lighted patio area. Before he could open his mouth to protest, a group of men appeared on the other side of the black iron gate that surrounded the pool. Seeing they were all fully clothed with the exception of one, Storm realized what this was. *Ain't this some television* The Sopranos-*ass shit?* His meeting was going to take place in the pool. Lowering his body into the cool water, he swam to the middle. When he came up for air, the man from the other end was there.

"Storm?"

"Yeah, that's me."

"A mutual friend seems to think you have what it takes to come aboard our little organization, so here I am."

"Yeah, I'm glad because thangs been kinda tight around my way."

"Trust me. We already know what's been going on with you and yours." The man bobbed around in the water like a child's float. "That's why we had you meet us out here, away from the city, in this pool, to make sure you weren't wearing a wire or no ridiculous shit like that. We don't like to take unnecessary risks. You understand, don't you?"

"Look," Storm tried reasoning with sincerity, "I ain't with no dumb shit! Everything I do is completely above board! My credibility is official."

"Okay, okay, stop politicking! You ain't running for office. If our man Rasul, back in Detroit, vouches for you being good people, then you good people. And, for the record, all them shootouts, territory beefs, the cops watching your ass, and that bullshit with Javier, we don't give a sweet fuck about that. That ain't our business or concern. You understand?"

"All right, cool." Storm was relieved his jaded past in the game wasn't gonna dictate his future.

"Listen up! We gonna make sure you laced with the strongest uncut product we can get across the border and through customs, but if you fuck up the ticket even once, let alone consider being late on the deadline, then you fucking out. No second chances. No 'cry me a river' excuses, you understand?" Sternly he looked Storm directly in the eye. "And depending how short or how late you are, you might end up dead! So if you truly not ready for the position we offering, I advise you, don't take it. We run a zero-tolerance operation!"

"Naw, naw." Storm moved his arms, making small ripples in the water. "I'm good, money. I'm with it. I'm ready! I'm your man!"

"Okay, so you say; but remember, Storm, don't get burned by the flame of the hustle. That shit can get hot at times, real fucking hot! When you get this package, as soon as your feet hit the ground, they better be running. The streets ain't waiting, and neither are we."

"No doubt, I understand."

"Well, since you a rookie with our team, you can expect a simple text every morning reminding you of your financial commitment to the family. Nothing more, nothing less."

Ultimately agreeing to the various strict terms put in place, Storm knew for certain that, with the aid of his little brother O.T., he'd soon be back on his feet making more than enough money to keep Kenya happy in Gucci and Prada, support his soon-to-be-born son, and get his stash back up to finish remodeling and reopening Alley Cats. Life was about to take a drastic change for the better.

The forty-minute drive returning to his car was a lot different from when they'd first come. After seeing what he was working with, especially in the dick department, his female escort, who finally announced her name was Anika, couldn't stop blabbing. Realizing Storm was now a part of the crew and would be soon definitely pulling in major figures to match that major-size manhood in his pants, in her eyes he'd just become a lot more interesting.

Storm hardly spoke a single word; instead, his mind was all over the place. From still wanting to get with Kenya for talking that bold shit about his soon-to-be-born son, to wondering when the next time Marco Meriwether was gonna show his black dreadlocked ass up, he stared out the tinted window of the Challenger up at the street lights. His thoughts bounced back and forth between the seven-day deadline he was just given to make his first payment and the fact that the high-quality product was waiting for him at a secret stash house he already had the key and address to. Ignoring the meaningless conversation coming out Anika's mouth, Storm looked at his watch not needing or wanting her friendship at this point. His main objective now was to get back to his ride so he could check in with O.T. and let him know it was on like hot butter popcorn! Soon they'd be back living and eating like kings. Nothing else mattered.

By the time the pair finally arrived back to the abandoned factory where Storm left his car parked, a socially unpolished Anika had already written her cell number down on the back of an old business card.

"Here you go. Call me when you bored." She winked handing it to him. "We's family now and remember: nightfall to day, them boys don't play. Have that ticket proper."

"I got this. Plus, I thought you had a man," Storm sarcastically replied getting out the Challenger and heading toward his own vehicle.

"And your point? Family is family!" She snickered before peeling off and out of sight.

Stuffing the card in his wallet, Storm hit his alarm system unlocking the doors. Before bothering to start the engine, he reached over on the passenger seat for his cell. *Damn, no missed calls?* He frowned knowing he'd been MIA for hours and no one had checked on his whereabouts. *Not from my brother or Kenya's angry ass. Fuck it!* Living in the celebration, thinking about how the new package was gonna change his already high-profile lifestyle, Storm pulled out of the dark, deserted lot. Trying both O.T.'s and Kenya's cells and receiving their voicemails repeatedly, he eagerly decided to drive to the new stash house solo. After all, he had seven short days to either shit or get off the pot and time was ticking.

Seconds from jabbing the blade through the boy's soft, tender skin, the piercing sounds of the ambulance siren driving off circulated throughout the living room. The blaring noise caused her to drop the knife from her hands. Kenya stood motionless by the couch still staring downward. The baby seemed to smile at her as his tiny mucus-covered body lay exposed. "This ain't right; this just ain't right." She came to her senses picking the little one up in her arms. "I done fucked up," she whispered, "but I can make it right. I promise you that, but we just can't be here when Storm gets home. I know he's not gonna understand I just let my sister die. Damn, even I don't understand."

Quickly deciding what to do, first things first, Kenya ran to the linen closet grabbing a few sheets and a wash-cloth. Letting the water in the kitchen sink get slightly warm, she bathed her crying nephew, washing off of all the fluids that coated his tiny body. Wrapping him snugly in an oversized towel, she stepped over London, placing him back on the couch next to the thick stack of legal papers and insurance policies Storm had underhandedly prepared. Pushing them to the floor with an "out of sight, out of mind" attitude, she remained focused on the infant's small voice.

Damn, you must be hungry. Kenya's mind was racing as she reasoned what exactly to do next to soothe his cries. Looking back and forth from her deceased sister to the baby, her first mind was the milk that undoubtedly was still inside of London's breasts. *Maybe I could let him suck on them?* Kenya desperately wondered placing her palm on her forehead as she looked at the wall clock. *Shit, I gotta make some sort of move quick before Storm gets here. I gotta think! Damn!* Kenya left the baby cry-ing on the couch and hit the remote, turning on another CD to temporarily drown out the sound. *I know him or that goddamn O.T. gonna show they punk asses up at any minute to check on London, so from this point on it gotta be whatever.*

Heading upstairs she grabbed her cell phone off the landing where she'd dropped it when the random gunfire first began. Staring down at the screen, her first instinct was to just call Storm and fess up, but the "I don't give a fuck about you no more" way he'd been acting lately and then lying about other shit, especially when it came to her twin sister, she couldn't trust him not to bug out and blame her. Yet, Storm calling the police on her was the last thing on her twisted mind. After all, Kenya had so much dirt on him and his brother that if she went down for jack shit, his ass and O.T. would come tumbling right down behind her; then, his oh-so-beloved son would have nobody but the foster care system in his life. Storm hurt her, so now she'd hurt him back. Now he could have his turn to see how it felt to be on the outside looking in for once.

Already having most of London's belongings thrown in the middle of the floor, Kenya searched through the pile picking out baby outfits that her sister and O.T. had purchased weeks before in anticipation of her giving birth. With the price tag still attached, Kenya grabbed a diaper bag, filling it with clothes and stuffing it with all the newborn Pampers that could fit inside. Not being able to close the zipper, she opened the closet to get another bag or suitcase out. Before she could pull out the black small-sized bag on wheels, a case of Similac was staring her in the face. *Hell yeah! Ain't this some shit? Good looking out, London, on always being so damn prepared!* Throwing a few cans of the formula in the suitcase, along with some bottles, Kenya rolled the bag to the edge of the stairs. She also took her sister's purse and cell phone off the charger stuffing it in her back pocket.

Going into the bedroom that she and Storm shared, she wasted no time entering the huge walk-in closet that she had specially built. Taking two huge Coach duffle bags and one Gucci makeup case out of the corner, Kenya snatched outfit after outfit down, some with the hangers still on, stuffing them into the bags. Frantically running back and forth to look out the window, it was as if the house were on fire and she'd been given five minutes to gather up her most prized possessions or lose them forever. When both of the duffle bags were packed to capacity, Kenya's hands clutched the straps, dragging them out of the bedroom and over near the bags with the baby's belongings.

Rushing back in the room and to her dresser, Kenya used her forearm to clear all her personal items off and into her oversized makeup case. Opening the top drawer, she grabbed a few pair of panties and bras. Kneeling at the side of the bed she slept on, Kenya raised the designer comforter reaching her hand underneath and removing a boot box that contained several pictures and important documents she couldn't bear to leave behind. Going to their stash spot, Kenya threw all her jewelry, Storm's jewelry, and close to $12,000 in cash into her purse. *He don't need none of this. Thanks to my dumb ass he about to get on! He can replace it! Twelve stacks ain't shit!* She felt no regrets for taking every watch, ring, and chain Storm owned, or the loot.

That's it, I guess. She paused as her eyes quickly scanned the room that she and the man of her dreams once shared. *Motherfuckers always saying you can't change a ho into a housewife; well, I guess you can't change a cheating-ass street nigga into a husband.* Infuriated she was forced to abandon all the rest of her clothes, some personal items that couldn't fit into her car, and the home she'd put so much of herself into, Kenya smashed a picture of her and Storm against the wall shattering the glass frame. *He wanna see a real Detroit diva in action, well, I'm that bitch!* Kenya hit the light switch with malice in her heart and revenge on her mind.

Out of breath, Kenya finally got the last bag loaded into her car. Feeding the baby a quick bottle to get him to stop crying, she went back upstairs snatching several fluffy bath towels out of the hamper. Placing them in a blue laundry basket, she carried it out to the attached garage. *Okay, this shit right here is gonna definitely work.* Keeping a close eye on the front door, Kenya started to worry as to why Storm hadn't come back yet from his meeting and why O.T.'s loud ass hadn't been around all day. *Maybe they ho asses is together celebrating the shit I made happen, whatever! Fuck 'em both!* The clock was ticking, and she knew sooner rather than later one of them was destined to show up, so she had to pick up the pace.

Taking the sleeping baby off the couch, Kenya had tears in her eyes as she placed her nephew on the floor next to his dead mother, her twin sister. "Sorry, y'all, but it's time for you two to say y'all good-byes." Leaving the room to make a call and give the pair a strange moment of privacy, Kenya wanted to throw up. She'd been involved in some pretty fucked-up bullshit since first meeting Storm, hell, really since she'd started dancing back home at Heads Up in Detroit; but leaving her sister's dead body in the middle of the floor took the cake. *Fuck Storm; he was just some dick when it came down to it. Granted it was good dick, but still just some dick.* However, London was her sister, her twin, her blood, and now she was treating her no better than she would a common ho in the street. *Shit! Fuck! Damn! God,* she silently prayed, *you gotta forgive me for this! Damn!*

Scrolling down the numbers in her cell phone contact list, Kenya found the name she was looking for. After two to three rings the man answered.

"Hey, Kenya."

"Hey. I need you to do me a favor."

"Anything, just name it."

"Thanks. I knew I could count on you. I need you to meet me at my friend's apartment in about twenty minutes. Can you make it?"

"Sure, you know I'm here for you and yours!"

Giving him the directions and other information he needed to know before meeting her there, Kenya ended the conversation telling him to keep their plans hush-hush.

Spending time at the house that hid his strong, uncut shipment of heroin, Storm tried calling his little brother once more. *Damn, where in the hell this nigga at?* he wondered as he figured out a game plan to move the illegal product as quickly and police drama–free as possible. Ol' boy in the swimming pool made it crystal clear that the ticket was nonnegotiable and the time frame for repayment was set in stone. *He probably somewhere laid up or rubbing his goddamn hands on my baby momma's stomach.* Storm fought with being jealous of the obvious bond his brother had seemed to build with London and his unborn son. *If I find out that nigga fucking her ass with my seed still in there . . . Naw, he wouldn't do that foul bullshit. But just to be on the safe side I'ma give his ass so much of this magic potion to move out in them streets, he gonna be too busy to worry about pussy, especially London's.*

Securing the stash house until he could make other arrangements to move the dope to another location in the morning, Storm jumped in his ride with a smile of satisfaction on his face. Keeping the radio low, he called O.T. a third and fourth time and was still met with the annoying, long, drawn-out musical message greeting on his voicemail. "I should call Kenya and see what's up, but I know she still tripping out about that insurance mess. Fuck it. London know where that nigga at, if nobody else do." After talking himself outta calling his fiancée, he called London's cell. *Damn, it's ringing. Shit! Her voicemail too!* Storm wasn't that far from the house, so he decided to just go home and face whatever dumb shit Kenya was gonna be talking as soon as he stepped inside. He'd been with her long enough to know that if his pockets were deep enough, he could buy her forgiveness for just about anything.

Within twenty minutes, he bent the corner of the gated community he called home. Noticing yellow tape around the spot where the fire hydrant was at and a street signpost lying on the side of the curb, Storm chalked it up to one of his many Caucasian neighbors who came home drunk on the regular knocking over any- and everything in their path. As he turned on his block, Storm drove past a car parked a few houses down from his that looked like O.T's, but he wasn't certain. Turning up in his driveway, he noticed the lights were all off except for a small glimmer shining through the security window of the front door. "Damn, where in the fuck is everybody?" He spoke under his breath knowing the darkness at this time of the evening was strange for his household.

KENYA
Going back into the living room, her heart broke as she bent down using her sister's cell phone to take a picture of her dead sister and the baby together. Fighting not to have another emotional breakdown Kenya exhaled. *Y'all both look like y'all sleeping.* As luck would have it, the cell rang no sooner than the picture was snapped. *Damn look at this bullshit! This nigga calling to check on his ho! He ain't shit!* An unexpected call from Storm to London set Kenya's emotions back into high gear. Picking up the child, she took him out to her car putting him in the laundry basket that was now doubling as a car seat.

On her final trip back inside the condo, Kenya lifted both her sister's legs and struggled dragging her out to the kitchen, past the storage room, and into the rear walk-in freezer leaving her by a case of porterhouse steaks. *Bye, sis. Tell Gran hi for me, 'cause I know I ain't making it to heaven.* Holding a solemn final conversation with her twin, Kenya made her peace before throwing a few Glade air fresheners inside. Shutting the freezer door behind her, she knew Storm wouldn't immediately discover London since he hated to cook, let alone defrost shit. Nine outta ten times, he wouldn't smell death in the usually vanilla-scented condo air. Nevertheless, Kenya hoped she was buying herself some time as she used several old rags and T-shirts to clean up the bloody remnants of the afterbirth spilled onto the living room floor. *Good, it's all up! No one can tell!* She tossed the rags underneath the sink as quickly as possible.

With car keys in hand, she headed toward the garage to leave her old life behind. *Oh my God! What in the entire hell!* She stopped dead in her tracks as a pair of bright headlights, unfortunately, pulled up in the driveway. *Shit! Fuck! Hell naw; not now of all damn times.* Seeing Storm jump out of the car, Kenya panicked running to get the same butcher knife she'd used to help deliver his son. Her heart was racing in anticipation of what was about to pop off. *Damn, what am I doing? But what will he say? He don't give a fuck about me! I gotta look out for me!* She argued with herself, sweaty palms and fingers tightening up on the handle of the sharp-edged knife. Biting her lips, Kenya took a deep breath as Storm came toward the front door of the condo.

"If he comes in here with that bullshit, I'm straight cutting his cheating ass," Kenya swore with every step Storm took up the walkway. "He started the shit, so I'm gonna finish it!" she reasoned trying to convince herself what she was gonna do if he didn't come correct.

"Oh, boy, here the fuck we go." Storm shook his head getting prepared for the drama that his girl was probably about to bring. Reaching his hand up to the screen door, he pulled at it, but it was locked. Still holding his keys, he searched through them finding the correct one. Sticking it in the lock, he turned the cylinder all the way to the right.

With her ear pressed to the door, Kenya's hand and arm shook, and her heart raced. She waited, knowing she was as good as caught. *Oh my God. I'ma have to just give him a hard gut shot with this knife and get it over with.*

Storm slowly opened the screen while looking through his keys for the right one to unlock the main door. Just as he found the right key and was sticking it in, he was interrupted by a voice calling out to him from the sidewalk.

"Excuse me! Excuse me! Mr. Christian, excuse me!" The same elderly neighbor who had knocked earlier, Mrs. Farrow, came closer. "How is your brother doing? Is he going to be okay?"

"Huh, my brother?" Storm paused still standing in between the two doors with his keys dangling from the lock. "What you mean is he going to be okay? I'm lost."

"I knocked at the door when it first happened, but no one came. You know we don't have that type of thing happen on our street or in this community!" She had a condescending, holier-than-thou attitude as she spoke.

"When what first happened?" Storm stepped off the porch letting the screen door slowly close.

Kenya perched down, knife still in hand, trying to hear what her nosey neighbor was saying but she couldn't quite make it out.

"When did this happen?" Storm shouted out confused at what he'd heard. "Are you sure?" He looked over at the car parked in front of her house that he thought was O.T.'s.

Seconds after his neighbor told him her colorful version of all the evening events that resulted in his little brother being shot in her driveway, Storm ran back up to the condo door snatching his keys out the lock, jumped back in his car, and peeled off en route to the hospital. "That must be where Kenya and London are both at. Dang, no wonder ain't nobody answering they cells." He pressed his foot down onto the accelerator not knowing his brother's medical condition or that he was now a father of a healthy baby boy. "Damn! That motherfucker dreadlock-wearing faggot gonna pay for this bullshit!" Storm banged on the steering wheel, automatically assuming Marco Meriwether had shot his brother.

Kenya said, "I wonder what in the fuck that old nosey-ass bitch told him now. With her, it's always something, but nine outta ten it was probably about some shit she ain't have no business telling in the first place! One day that nosey shit gonna get her face smacked off. She lucky I'm on a mission, or I would do it my-damn-self."

Relieved Storm didn't come inside and strangely chose to drive off like his ass was on fire, Kenya ran out to the garage to make her getaway before he came back.

Chapter Three

KENYA

"Hey what up, doe? What took you so long to get here?" Kenya peeked out Paris's apartment door to make sure her visitor was alone. "I was starting to think you stood me up."

"Never that." Big Doc B barely fit between the small space that Kenya had left in between herself and the doorway. "I was at the club and had to go back by the house and grab my bag."

"Oh, okay then." Kenya smiled while still trying to fix her nappy hair. "You gotta excuse the way I look, but I've kinda been through it tonight."

"You always look good, Miss Lady. Storm is a lucky man," he respectfully commented even though he'd never seen Kenya in sweats before. "I've always told him that."

"Whatever," Kenya offhandedly remarked while leading him to the rear area of the apartment and into the bedroom.

"Is O.T. here? This is his place if I remember correctly isn't it?"

Stopping him in the hallway, just before entering the bedroom, Kenya was over being cordial. "Look, man, what's with all the twenty questions and shit? Ain't nobody here but me and I need you to do me a favor. Now are you with it or not?" With her hands posted on her hips, she waited for his reply.

Big Doc B didn't want any problems with Kenya because he knew ultimately that meant problems with Storm and that was definitely a headache no one in the city wanted. "I'm sorry, Miss Lady, I was just—"

"Naw, we good, Doc." Kenya changed her tone quickly realizing she could get more honey from any man being sweet. "My bad; just come on and hook a sister up." She made sure she rubbed her body against his.

Stepping into the room, Big Doc B saw a baby clad in a small blanket resting in the center of the king-sized bed. "Is something wrong with the child?"

Taking a deep breath, Kenya started telling him the lie she'd concocted on the drive over. "Well, it's like this. One of the dancers from Alley Cats called me." She rubbed her sweaty palms together as she continued to lie. "Apparently she was pregnant and didn't know it."

"Oh, yeah? Wow!" Listening attentively to Kenya, Doc unwrapped the blanket, examining the infant.

"Yeah, and her man didn't know she was knocked up either!" Kenya watched Doc's face to see if he was buying her fabricated story so far. "She told me her dude can't have any kids so he would know she was fucking the next nigga if she would've kept the baby. She texted me to meet her at a motel off the interstate and this—I mean, he"—she pointed at the baby—"is what I found."

Seeing the child's umbilical cord was still attached, Big Doc B reached inside his medical bag. A plastic surgeon by trade, scalpels and other sharp instruments were his specialty. "I can fix him up, but you sure you don't want to take him through emergency?"

"No!" Kenya yelled causing her sleeping nephew to jump. "She might get in trouble. I promised her!"

"Don't worry, Kenya, I got you." As he clipped the cord properly, his mind started to wonder exactly what dancer was the mother of this baby he was helping. "Listen, I'm not trying to overstep my boundaries, and you and Storm know I'd never open my mouth, but which girl—"

Kenya wasn't dumb. She figured out where he was going with his statement and stopped him. "Don't worry, Doc; it ain't one of your favorites. I swear to God you good."

Relieved one of the young dancers he often tricked with, especially Jordan, an ex-dancer at Alley Cats, hadn't given birth to his illegitimate child and he would be forced to tell his prescription-addicted, pill-popping wife, Doc smiled. "Oh, I was just thinking, that's all." He went to the bathroom to wash his small scalpel off and get a warm rag to finish cleaning the baby up.

Kenya looked at her small nephew lying on the bed and knew she needed some extra insurance if she wanted to keep Doc from mentioning the baby to Storm or O.T., even in passing. Removing her sweatshirt, Kenya rubbed her breasts, causing the nipples to get hard and poke out through the white wife beater that hugged her body. Taking her vibrating cell phone out of her back pocket, she saw she had an incoming call from Paris's physician. *Wrong time for updates. Whatever's wrong with her is just wrong! Leave a fucking message!* Propping her phone on the dresser, Kenya asked, "So do you think he'll be okay without going to the hospital?"

When Doc reentered the bedroom to answer Kenya's question, he was shocked to see her headlights standing straight out. "Um, um, yeah, he's gonna be fine. But he does need to be cared for properly."

"Oh my God!" Kenya ran up to him wrapping her arms around his neck. "Thank you sooo much! I knew I could count on you!"

"Anytime." Doc was in heaven as Kenya hugged him tightly. Being the freak he was, automatically his dick started to get hard. "Not a problem." He tried backing away from her grip, but couldn't.

Hell yeah, I'm on now. Kenya felt his manhood stiffening. Reaching her hand down, she started stroking it through his Dockers. "Damn, it's like that?"

"I'm so sorry, Kenya." He pulled back stumbling against the wall and dropping the scalpel to the floor. "I apologize."

"For what?" Kenya smiled licking her lips. "For being human? For seeing something you like?"

Doc's dick got harder by the second as he tried to explain. "No, it's not that."

"Then what?" She raised the wife beater exposing her bare breasts. As each hand groped her breasts, Doc's eyes danced around not knowing what to do next. "You don't like what you see?"

"Yesss, but Storm—"

Wasting no time with what he was going to say next, Kenya, turned into Tastey and dropped to her knees, unbuckled his belt, and unzipped the middle-aged man's pants. Shockingly surprised to discover his dick was at least half an inch longer than Storm's, she started to slobber on the head then suck him off until he busted. It had been way over a year since she had any other man's dick in her mouth, except for Storm, but she was on a mission. When she finally let go of Doc's dick, he was panting trying to stay balanced on his feet.

"Kenya, please don't tell Storm! If he ever found out, he'd kill me! Please!"

"We friends now ain't we?" Kenya stood to her feet walking over to the dresser. Picking up her cell phone, she excused herself going into the living room. "I'll be right back."

Moments later, Big Doc B bolted out the rear bedroom waving his phone. "Why? I don't understand! Why would you record that? Why?"

"Oh, I see you got my little message, huh?" Kenya smiled as Doc's hand fumbled trying to delete the video of her sucking his dick. "I thought you'd want a reminder of our newfound friendship!"

"My wife! Storm! Please erase that, Kenya, please!" Holding his hand up to his open mouth he panicked accidently pressing play again on the video. "You trying to get me killed or something? If Storm ever found out—"

"Don't worry, sweetie." She seductively walked over caressing his face with one hand while rubbing his now limp pipe with the other. "As long as you don't tell anyone about me being over here let alone even seeing that baby back there, you good!" She then strutted toward the door. "But if you mention a single solitary word to anybody and it gets back to me, Storm gonna get to see a copy of our award-winning performance! Shit, then you know he gonna kill you and probably your entire damn family! You know how my man gets down when he's angry, don't you?"

"Yeah, I know." Seeing firsthand Storm, O.T., and their ruthless cohorts stump the piss out of more than a few unruly guys down at Alley Cats, Big Doc B dropped his head knowing he would forever be silent if he wanted to live.

Before turning the doorknob, Kenya stuck out her hand. "Oh, by the way, any cash you got on you I'm gonna need. So please run it!" Big Doc B, dumbfounded, took out his wallet giving her all $653 he had inside. Kenya noticed his gas card and took that also. "Thanks, Doc! And for the record, if I weren't bleeding, I would've got some of that big-ass dick of yours! Your wife is the lucky one!" Kenya shut the door in his face leaving Doc confused as hell, scared shitless, and most definitely satisfied like a motherfucker with her impromptu blowjob.

Not knowing O.T. was battling for his life, Tangy was dead, and Paris was about to confess all of their deadly secrets to anyone who would listen, Kenya went on with her game plan to get out of dodge. Gathering a few additional items at the apartment she might need on the long road trip ahead, Kenya and the baby she nicknamed Li'l Stone after her dead uncle got on their way. Getting a full tank of gas, courtesy of Big Doc B, and a huge bag of sour cream and onion potato chips, she drove to the highway heading toward home: Detroit.

Passing a police squad car, Kenya got nervous, feeling remorseful for all of twenty seconds before the guilt left her system all together. *Fuck this town!* If all went as planned, Kenya and "her newborn son" would be back in the Motor City in nineteen hours.

PARIS
Within a few hours of O.T. leaving her bedside, Paris started mumbling different words and shaking as if she was going into convulsions. Doctors, as well as the nurses on staff, were in shock because, up until now, the once beautiful, outgoing girl hadn't spoke since being transferred there.

"Dead!" Disoriented she sat straight up in her hospital gown shouting out as her eyes bucked twice their normal size. "Blood!"

"Do you hear the awful things she's saying?" one nurse asked the other as they tried stabilizing her.

"Blood. Dead. Blood!" Paris's voice rang throughout the normally quiet facility. "Deacon! Deacon!" Her hands wrung together at a fast pace.

"Oh, my." The second nurse closed her sweater tightly standing by the window. "One can only wonder what this poor child has been through."

"You're right," the nurse answered holding their patient's legs as still as possible. "Maybe that's why she tried committing suicide. Whatever it is, it's weighting heavy on that child's heart that's for sure."

"Baby. Bunny. Dead. Baby!" The words got clearer and extremely louder. "Sorry. Sorry. Sorry!"

As Paris continued to ramble on not making any sense whatsoever, the doctor finally entered giving her a mild sedative to calm her down. "Keep an eye on her pressure and monitor her heart rate as well."

"Dead! Dead! Blood!" Through dry and cracked lips, Paris sporadically screamed out a few more confused, troubling words before the shot took an almost immediate effect and she closed her eyes.

Standing outside of the private room, the two nurses explained to the doctor that Paris's abrupt erratic behavior started shortly after a visit from a young man earlier that day. "One minute he was sitting in the chair near her bedside talking and the next he ran out of the front entranceway like a bat outta hell!" Both caregivers agreed as they looked over Paris's chart.

Taking into consideration the off-color remarks Paris was saying, the doctor, who was also the head of the facility, made the determination to contact his patient's next of kin who was listed, Tangelina Gibson, and Kenya James and, most importantly, the police detective who had months prior come inquiring about Paris's overall mental state wanting to question her pertaining to some unsolved homicide cases. The doctor got no answer from either of the women, but Sergeant Kendricks picked up, incidentally informing the doctor he was already en route to the facility to serve Paris a death notification of her cousin.

STORM

Rushing through the double emergency room doors, Storm was met by two uniformed security guards before he could get to the information desk. "Yo, my little brother is back there." He tried to bulldoze his way by. "Get the fuck outta my way! Get the fuck on!"

"Listen, guy." The heavyset guard shoved back as his partner placed his hand on his firearm. "Unless you go through that metal detector and then calm down, I don't care if Jesus is passing out autographed Bibles on the other side of this wall, you ain't getting by!"

Trying to regain his composure so he could see what exactly was going on with O.T., Storm took a deep breath. "Look, y'all. I just found out they brought my people in here with gunshot wounds! I need to get back there, ASAP!"

"A black male? Did he come by way of ambulance or do you know?" The armed guard over to the side looked on, questioning and hoping to expedite and defuse the situation.

"Yeah." Storm's face showed signs of worry as sweat poured off his brow. "Sometime this damn evening! Now I gotta go see him!"

After the two guards quickly exchanged glances, they hurried to get Storm through the checkpoint, while again advising him to calm down. Moments later the receptionist was calling a doctor out to the desk to speak to Storm regarding O.T.'s medical condition.

"Excuse me, sir, but are you the family of Othello Terrence Christian?"

"Yes, he's my brother!" Storm almost knocked the doctor off his feet and his clipboard to the floor as he ran to his side. "Can I see him? Is he good? You need to take me to him!"

"I'm sorry, but he's still in surgery. It seems like there was extensive damage to some vital organs and he lost an enormous amount of blood. Unfortunately, it's going to be awhile, but I'll keep you updated."

Left standing in limbo, feeling like his world had just ended, Storm's eyes searched the packed waiting room area for Kenya and London, who he assumed both had to be there. Not seeing either, he reached on his hip for his cell phone to once again dial Kenya, but he was interrupted by an unwanted face approaching him. "What in the fuck do you want?"

"Storm, how you doing? Not too good, huh?" Gloating over Storm's misery, Detective Malloy answered his own question.

"Dude, what the fuck you want? I ain't got time for no bullshit!"

"Any news on O.T.?" He nodded his head toward the doorway going to the back. "He didn't look so good when they brought him in. At least that's what word on the street is!"

"Fuck the word on the street, you feel me?" Storm's fist closed tightly and his teeth clenched together as he spoke. "And, matter of fact, dig this here, Dudley Do-Right house nigga, ain't jack shit about my brother your fucking business, all right?" He licked his lips sticking his chest out. "Instead of being all up here in mines, you should be out trying to find Marco's ho ass before I catch that grimy son of a bitch and kneecap him for good!"

Detective Malloy easily read in between the lines and happily enlightened Storm with an update to his misinformed belief. "Marco? You mean Marco Meriwether? Man, we picked him up early this afternoon at the Greyhound bus station at least a good ten or so miles away from the location your brother took them slugs at!"

Storm was obviously confused, and it showed. "Come on, guy, don't play with me. What is you trying to say?"

"You know Tangelina Gibson?" He stepped to Storm with a crooked grin. "Well, that manly carpet-muncher is the one who tried to take your little brother out the game. A goddamn female! Now ain't that a kick in the ass!"

"Tangy?" Storm was stunned to hear her name. "I thought that dyke was locked the fuck up; now you saying she the one who shot my little brother?"

"Yeah, she shot him. Chased him down like a dog!" The detective laughed at her nerve. "But karma kicked in faster than she thought. One of our guys had to kill her, so I guess you kinda owe the department, huh?"

"What?" Storm backed up fighting with himself not to swing on the mouthy cop.

"Yeah, we saved you a bullet and a murder case!" Detective Malloy smiled as he glanced down reading a text message from his partner Sergeant Kendricks.

"Man, get the fuck on!" Storm had just about enough of Malloy's slick comments. "I ain't trying to hear shit you talking!"

"Not a problem. It's all good; duty calls anyway! It seems like your brother's little girlfriend, Paris Peterson, is out at the nuthouse all of a sudden in the talking mood! Go figure!" He casually strolled to the exit. "Maybe I'll be back to see you after we talk to her and see what interesting things she has to say. What you think? You'll be here right?" Being a sarcastic asshole, Detective Malloy left.

That Negro is straight working my motherfucking nerves. One day I'ma lay that fag and his partner out, badge or not! And Paris best to keep that mouth of hers shut about me and mines! Watching one of the constant thorns in his side leave, Storm made his way all the way inside the packed waiting area to make sure he hadn't overlooked Kenya's and London's presence. *Damn, they ain't here. Maybe they went to grab something to eat or some shit like that.* "But why Kenya ain't at least call me? I know she probably still pissed the fuck off, but shit!" he mumbled under his breath calling her cell once more.

"You've reached 313-443—"

Storm hung up after hearing the recorded message on Kenya's cell. Taking a seat near the vending machines, he quietly waited for his fiancée and her sister, his baby momma, to return. Considering the fact that Marco's spiteful ass was knocked on the bus way before the last time he'd spoken to Kenya, Storm wasn't overly worried about where either twin was at. *That nosey old bitch, Mrs. Farrow, and Malloy's ho ass only know so much of what jumped off at the crib. When Kenya gets back, hopefully she can tell me the real deal.* Leaning his head back, Storm shut his eyes daydreaming about the good old days. The ones when he and O.T. were just kids and their mother wasn't sucking on a glass dick and sticking a needle in every vein she could find.

Chapter Four

BROTHER RASUL

Ring. Ring.

"Hey, Kenya, what's going on, sis?" Brother Rasul grabbed the remote control pausing the DVD he and Fatima were watching.

"I really, really messed up this time!" Kenya yelled into the phone as she drove in the darkness of the highway. "I don't know if even you can forgive me this time!"

"Come on now, Kenya, you know me and you go way back. Ain't nothing strong enough to break what me and you have. I'm always gonna be there."

Fatima was instantly infuriated hearing her man tell the next female how devoted he was to her. She knew Kenya was selfish and self-serving, not to mention London was her best friend in the world and she hated the way Kenya had been treating her. "What do she want now? With her it's always some damn drama!"

"Is that the television or do you have company?"

Brother Rasul wasn't in the mood for listening to Fatima badmouth his homegirl. Tossing the remote on the couch, he stood up going into the other room. "Naw, I'm good, Kenya. What's wrong? Did Storm handle his business or what?"

"I don't really know for sure." Kenya sighed wondering how things had gone berserk so quickly to the point of no return.

"What you mean you don't know?" Brother Rasul opened the refrigerator taking out a bottle of apple juice. "He should have been back from the meeting by now."

"Can you please stop talking about him and listen to me?" Kenya insisted before coming up on the next exit and pulling over to the side of the road. "I messed up, and I need you."

"Where you at now?" Brother Rasul twisted the cap off and took a quick swig. "What's all that noise? Are you outside?"

Kenya had to confide in someone and who better than the one person in her life next to Gran, Stone, and London who were all dead but always had her back regardless. "You gotta promise not to tell anyone you talked to me, okay? Please!"

"All right, not a problem." He raised his eyebrow taking another swallow.

"I mean it; not Storm if he calls you and not even Fatima! Promise me, Brother Rasul! I'm serious!"

"Look, I already gave you my word, and you know it's bond. Now, what's wrong, sis?"

Kenya was ready to confess. The burden of what she'd done was weighing heavy on her conscience. As the tears started to flow, she explained to him that she was in her car and on her way driving across state back to Detroit. "No matter what you might hear about me in the next few hours, until I get there, don't believe it!" she begged, wiping her tears with the side of her hand. "When I see you I'll explain!"

"All right, li'l sis." He could only imagine what bullshit Kenya had gotten herself into now, but whatever it was he was definitely gonna stick by her.

"Remember you promised and you the only one I can trust!" Kenya looked over her shoulder at her sleeping little rear-seat passenger as she headed back toward the entrance ramp. "I'll be there as soon as I can."

"I got you. Be safe and check in with me along the way." Closing his cell phone, Brother Rasul went back in the den where Fatima was still sitting on the couch. Reaching for the remote, he restarted the movie not saying a word about the strange call.

"Oh, hell naw!" Fatima shouted jumping to her feet. "That's it? Just like that? You gonna take her damn call then leave out the room like y'all got some old top-secret bullshit going on? How you playing me?"

"Who are you addressing like that, Fatima?" Once again he stopped the movie. "I never disrespect you; and the fact that you think you can verbalize to me in that tone, in my house no less, you have a major problem! We have a major problem!"

Fatima had enough of the Kenya/Brother Rasul show that was always going on, and she decided to finally speak her mind. "You need to cut her off! I'm sick and tired of her always calling you for this, that, and the third! She got a man! He might be a cheating sack of shit, but that's her choice! Now when is it gonna stop? Why you so devoted to his damn woman?"

"Now it's for you to demand who I cut off, who I help, and who I'm loyal to?" Brother Rasul, now pissed off and defensive, joined Fatima in the middle of the room. Standing six foot four with at least 285 pounds of muscle, he looked down at the younger woman he'd been dating. "Maybe it's time you reevaluate this relationship and your devotion! Know your place. The Quran says—"

"Listen, despite what you think, I ain't new to this! I know what the fuck it says!" She stomped her foot folding her arms as if she were a child having a tantrum. Wanting a reaction, she went all the way to the south. "Dudes kill me trying to make excuses for they foul-ass actions! Do you quote the Quran when you and the Motown Muslim Mafia decide to deal with motherfuckers? Huh? Hell naw, it might as well be the Bible then! So, nigga, please get on with all that!"

"Nigga? Nigga? Have you lost your senses?" Brother Rasul's biscuit brown skin turned one shade darker. With everything in his power, he fought not to collar Fatima up and smack some respect into her.

That was it for him, and Fatima knew it as well. She'd crossed the line in an attempt to make her point. With blood obviously in her man's eyes and a small vein on the side of his forehead sticking out, Fatima got her purse. Heading to the door then marching to her car while she was still in one piece, she kept pressing her luck. "For real, though, you need to take some time and figure out why you so much of a Captain Save A Ho whenever Kenya's fake ass involved! You can just call me when you can get rid of that lowlife strip-club dancing dirt bag!" She waited to get a safe distance between him and her before she got any braver with her insults, stipulations, and claims. "I'm over the games, nigga!" She stressed every letter in the word.

"You know what, Fatima, you might need to come back in here and pack all your belongings because I don't take orders from women, especially disrespectful ones who don't know their place!" He looked from side to side to see if any of his neighbors were out listening to her rants and accusations.

"Naw, Rasul, I tell you what! You can just burn all my stuff! I'm good! You's a fake-ass Muslim!" Fatima, calling herself a strong black woman, refusing to shed a tear, threw his spare house keys onto the grass and sped out of the driveway.

Brother Rasul retrieved the keys then slammed his front door shut. Infuriated about the way he was spoken to and disrespected, he went to the bathroom leaning over the white porcelain sink. Splashing cold water on his face to calm down, he took Fatima's advice when he rose up staring into the mirror. *Damn, why do I always put my neck on the line for Kenya's crazy ass?* He used his hand wiping down the wetness from his angry mug. *Why?*

STORM
Having fallen asleep in the waiting area, Storm was awakened from his dream-turned-nightmare just as he was killing his stepfather. As his heart rate pumped overtime and his adrenalin slowed down, his eyes opened to see a nurse with a handful of papers standing over him. "Damn, hey." Storm sat up from the scrunched position he was sitting in. "You got some news about my little brother?"

Nurse Jamison placed her hand on his shoulder. "Are you Tony Christian?"

"Yeah, that's me."

"Well, can you come with me? I want to talk to you in private."

"Yeah, of course." Storm stood to his feet shaking off the deep, troubling sleep he was just in.

"If you have any other family members down here, they are more than welcome to join us."

At that moment, it hit Storm like a ton of bricks that neither Kenya nor London had shown up to the emergency room. "Naw, I guess I'm here solo, so we can just go."

Following the nurse behind the otherwise secure triage area, Storm was led into a small, serenely decorated room with six leather chairs and a coffee table with a box of tissue sitting in the middle. "Please take a seat."

"Look, I'm not trying to be rude, but I've been down here for hours." Storm checked his watch for the time.

"I'ma need to see my brother. First y'all said he was in surgery; now y'all got me in this room. Quit trying to stale me out! What's the deal?"

Nurse Jamison felt his pain and decided to delete the formalities and cut to the chase. "Okay, Mr. Christian, I'm gonna be blunt with you. Your brother Othello is in extremely critical condition. The doctors are still doing what they can do; however, it's bad. I'm not gonna sugarcoat it for you." She took a seat next to Storm in an effort to console and hopefully ease his fears. "He definitely is gonna need several more procedures done before he's out of the deep end of the water, but his body needs time to heal from the more serious of the wounds just treated. He's being moved into a special trauma unit, and you can visit with him. But just keep in mind he's been through a lot and is extremely weak. You can sit with him, but be aware he is unconscious. He has a lot of machines and monitors in his room, so please don't be alarmed."

Storm took in everything she'd just said. "Thanks for breaking it all down to me. I appreciate you keeping it a hundred."

"Not a problem. I'm gonna take you to your brother now, but you can only see him briefly. They're preparing his recovery room, so he'll be moved almost immediately."

Storm slowly entered the dimly lit hospital room. Inhaling the overwhelming smell of disinfectant, mixed with sickness, he saw O.T. laid out with tubes and needles in every part of his body. *Damn, what the fuck!*

Noticing Storm's apprehensiveness, Nurse Jamison spoke up once again, touching his arm. "It's okay. He needs family. You've got to be strong for him."

In shock, Storm sat down next to O.T.'s bed. Reaching out, he held his brother's hand. "Yeah, dude, don't worry, that bitch Tangy is dead. The fucking police shut the ho down right after she shot you."

Upset seeing his only family fucked up, knocking at death's door, Storm posted up as long as he could. When the medical staff arrived to transfer O.T. to the other ward, Storm went back into the small private waiting area where he tried once again to reach Kenya.

KENYA / STORM

Having driven for hours, Kenya was exhausted. In between her guilty conscience and being concerned about Li'l Stone, she exited at a small motel to get some much-needed rest. Wiping the sleep out of her puffy red eyes, Kenya went to the front desk ringing the silver bell attached to the counter. Showing them London's ID and paying the thirty-five-dollar short stay fee, she was soon heading to her room. After opening the door and making sure no one was looking, Kenya took the laundry basket out of her rear seat taking the baby inside the mildew-odor-filled room. Carefully setting him on the bed, she then returned to the car getting the bag with his diapers and milk inside. Changing the infant's wet and soiled diaper, she made him a bottle running it under the hot water. As she rocked Li'l Stone in her arms while feeding him, Kenya used her other hand to take her cell phone out of her purse.

"Damn, I need to put this shit on the charger." She noticed she had barely one bar of power left. Flipping it open to call Brother Rasul and check in with him, she pushed SEND placing the phone to her ear. "Hello."

"Yeah, hello! Hello! Kenya!" Storm's strong baritone voice shouted through the earpiece. "Kenya! Hello!"

Stunned he was on the line, Kenya was frozen with fear. She wasn't ready to face him and what he was going to say. By now she knew he'd discovered the God-awful truth of what she'd done. *Oh, shit, damn!*

"Yo, I hear your ass breathing!" Storm was going hard not letting up. "Stop bullshitting with me. This ain't the time! I know you hear me don't you?"

Kenya stared down at Storm's son and stopped rocking. "Yeah, I hear you," she mumbled almost so low he had to press his finger against his eardrum to hear her voice.

"Look, I know you still pissed about that insurance bullshit, but that shouldn't stop you from being down here with me!"

The insurance papers? Why he saying that? Why ain't he talking about London?

"I mean, Kenya, baby, I know I was wrong not to tell you, but do I deserve this?"

"Huh?" Kenya questioned confused with where he was going with his conversation.

Storm, relieved she'd finally answered his call, laid everything out. "How you think I feel to be down here in this son of a bitch by myself?"

"By yourself? Down here?"

"Yeah, by myself! Who else was gonna be here?" After a few brief seconds of silence, Storm went on. "Where was you at when it happened?"

"When what happened?" Still focusing on the baby, who was now wide awake, Kenya hoped he wasn't being so nonchalant in asking where she'd let her sister die.

"Did you see that ho Tangy shoot him or what? Matter of fact, when the fuck did she get out of jail?"

"Tangy?" Kenya was really lost. "Did you say Tangy?"

"Yo, Kenya, what in the fuck is wrong with you? Why in the hell you keep answering my damn questions with questions? Is you high or something?"

"Naw, I'm not high. I was just—"

"Listen, it's obvious you don't give a fuck about that slimy-ass cousin of Paris shooting O.T., but I thought at least London cared. Why she ain't down here at the hospital with me?"

It was then that Kenya's stomach dropped to her knees. She exhaled as her chest went up and down feeling like a huge weight had been lifted. She started putting two and two together, quickly realizing that the loud barrage of gunfire on the block earlier must've been Tangy shooting. *Damn, when did that crazy bitch even get out?* she wondered as the wheels in her mind kept turning. *That's what that old, nosey-ass bitty told him. Oh my God! That was O.T.'s feet I saw in that fucking driveway!* "Listen, Storm," Kenya said, slowly easing the bottle from Li'l Stone's mouth seeing he had enough, "I had no idea Tangy would do something like that!"

"Whatever. At this point, it don't even matter 'cause the bitch is dead, but you still didn't say why y'all ain't down here and why you ain't try to get in touch with a nigga!"

He ain't even been to the crib! He don't know shit about London. "Well, I've been—"

Having had enough of the one-sided twenty questions game, an infuriated Storm asked to speak to London. "Let me speak to your sister. I wanna see why she ain't here checking for my brother she love so damn much!"

Hearing Storm put the words "London" and "love" together in the same sentence, Kenya's blood pressure started to rise. Standing up, she placed Li'l Stone on the bed. Closing her eyes tightly, she wished she could turn back the hands of time.

"Yo, Kenya! What the fuck! Did you hear me? I said put London on the phone. I'm tired of playing around with your childish ass!" he yelled as some of the hospital staff walked past the once quiet room he was occupying. "I'm under enough stress; now put London on!"

Three seconds short of having a nervous breakdown, Kenya paced the cheap motel room floor with her cell pressed to her ear. "Stop telling me what to do! You got me fucked up to keep asking about my sister! Why you so worried about her?"

"Because she's having my damn baby all right? So excuse the fuck outta me if I wanna talk to her! My brother is lying in the other room fighting for his life, and I want my people here with me! Is that too much for a nigga to ask?"

"Your people?" Kenya paused. "Is that what you said? Is she the only one you worried about?"

"Yeah, she's having my fucking baby, my flesh and blood, so yeah, I'm worried about her! Stop damn tripping!" Storm blurted out tired of walking on eggshells about London's controversial pregnancy. "And real motherfucking rap, at the end of the day no matter what silly shit you talking, he still my son and I ain't never not gonna be around him! So grow the fuck up and put your sister on the—"

Thank God Kenya's cell went dead in the middle of Storm's aggravated, inspired rant. Looking at her screen, which was now dark, she hissed his name in vain, tossing the cell onto the nightstand. Barely able to keep her weary eyes open she lay down on the bed talking to the baby. "That's messed up about O.T., but how he gonna be saying that bullshit to me about London? He wrong as hell!" Lifting her head up hearing her sister's cell phone vibrate twice inside her purse, Kenya smirked ignoring the two calls she knew were both from Storm.

"Hello! Hello!" Storm repeated not receiving an answer from his so-called girl. "I know that dumb, simple-minded bitch ain't just hang up on me again!" Knocking the box of tissue to the floor, he was over Kenya's games. Pissed, to say the least, he then dialed London's cell getting her voicemail. This time he left a message just to spite Kenya: "Yeah, hey, baby momma! I was just checking on you and my son. I don't know if ya jealous sister told you, but O.T. is hurt and needs you to come down here. Matter of fact we both need you, so call me or come on down." Before hanging up, he put the icing on the revenge-filled cake. "Oh, yeah, tell my son I love him more than anything or anybody on this earth!" *That will teach Kenya ass to say fuck me and my little brother!*

Chapter Five

It was the crack of dawn. Having faced one of the most confusing, troublesome, and tragedy-filled days of their lives each person in their twisted circle prayed for a new beginning.

PARIS
Sergeant Kendricks's lower back was killing him. After sleeping in the sparsely padded chair for hours in anticipation of Paris maybe once again speaking, giving him a small bit of a lead he and Malloy could use to possibly close a few open cases, he stood to his feet. Stretching his arms, Kendricks peered out the window. Adjusting his firearm that was tucked on his side holster, he called the stationhouse checking in.

"Naw, Malloy, she still unconscious. I've been out here all night and not a single word. But I did inform the staff to take her butch cousin off her emergency contact list. I'm gonna stay out here another few minutes and talk to the nurses who were on duty when she was doing all that talking and see what light they can shed."

"Yeah, okay, good. When you leave there get some shuteye. I'll catch up with you later and fill you in on what went down with Storm in detail."

"All right then, Malloy. Later." Ending the call, turning back around, Sergeant Kendricks once again stared into Paris's sleeping face wishing he were years younger and could actually pull a female like her, but he knew "bad bitches" were reserved for gangsta-style dudes like the ones he hunted on a regular.

KENYA

Awakened by the miniature sound of Li'l Stone's cries for a bottle, Kenya wiped her eyes feeling refreshed. Having slept off her anger for the things Storm was saying before her cell went dead, happily she gave her nephew what he was yearning for. As she fed him, she plugged her phone into the charger. Even though Kenya was dreading having to listen to another one of Storm's rages that was sure to follow when he got home and discovered she wasn't there and London was dead, she still needed her phone while on the road. Part of Kenya felt sorry for Storm having to deal with O.T. being shot on his own, and wanted to turn back, while the other part knew things between them could never be the same.

Burping the baby and rocking him back to sleep, Kenya turned on the shower in the low-budget motel waiting almost ten solid minutes before the water even got luke-warm. Feeling the wetness, Kenya let the flow spray from the nozzle as her emotions fought. After getting out and drying off, she was about ready to hit the highway once again. Searching through her purse for a comb or brush, she felt London's cell phone vibrate. *Damn, this still on.* Pushing the button on the side to light the screen, Kenya saw two missed calls: one from Fatima and one from Storm. In the corner, there was a small envelope with a circle around it indicating London also had voicemail. *I almost hate to hear what that nigga done said.* Her mind told her not to listen, but her curiosity, of course, got the best of her.

Three seconds in to listening to Storm's hurtful message, Kenya knew she'd made the right decision to say fuck him! Changing Li'l Stone's diaper, Kenya loaded him along with herself into the car and took off.

DEADLY ALLIANCES
7

With eyes still half closed, Storm lifted his head to read the text message from a random number he'd never seen before. Taking time to process what exactly that number meant, he soon realized it was the amount of days he had to make his initial payment on the product he'd just been blessed with. However, considering his brother, the main street hustler in the family, was on his back fighting to live, Storm automatically got a headache, knowing that blessing could easily turn into a curse. *Shit, all this is fucked up!* He went to the bathroom located a few yards from O.T.'s hospital bed. After taking a morning piss, Storm washed his hands regretting the message that he'd left London hoping Kenya wouldn't hear it. *I know Kenya ass is spoiled like a motherfucker, but that shit I left was cold.* The warm water loosened up his stiff hands he'd slept on. *But still, she and London should've come down here.*

Checking with the doctor, who promised O.T. was stabilized for the time being and out of immediate danger, Storm headed out the hospital and toward the location he'd parked his car the night before. "What the fuck?" Looking up at the signpost, which read Do Not Park Fire Zone Your Vehicle Will Be Towed, Storm couldn't believe his shady luck.

"Damn, I guess I need to catch a fucking cab to the damn crib and get Kenya's ass to get the car outta impound! That's the last time I'm putting a car in a ho's name!"

Beep! Beep!

Hearing the sound of a horn honk twice and the small candy apple red Toyota driving up, Storm cracked a half-crooked smile. "Whoa, girl, you right on time."

"Hey, Storm, I heard about O.T., so I came to sit with you and Kenya's evil-acting ass," Jordan announced, winking. "You know we family inside Alley Cats and out, even though ya girl fired me!"

"Damn good looking, J. I appreciate that shit!" Storm finally had someone in his presence who cared what he was going through. Sure, she had been just a dancer at his club and a troublemaker, but at least she showed up. "O.T. is holding his own. You know that nigga is a warrior. Can't shit shut him down!"

"Yeah, I know what you mean," Jordan remarked running her fingers through her long weave. "Is he up to visitors? Where is Kenya at? Is she still inside?"

Storm was snatched back to the reality that his woman was MIA. "Naw, she somewhere else right now. But, dig this here. These sons of bitches done towed my shit! Can you run me out to my spot?"

"Yeah, babe, jump in." Jordan, a bona fide flirt, made sure her miniskirt was pushed up as far as it would go so Storm could see her legs and the three-inch stilettos she was rocking at seven in the morning. Having never been to her ex-boss's house, she followed his directions. With every twist and turn, Jordan shifted her body as sexy as she could.

Storm had seen her swinging naked on a pole a hundred times over, so seeing her with clothes, skimpy as they might be, was of no big deal. Besides he had more important issues on his plate than a scheming female. "Make a right turn. The second street. Just past the light."

Jordan was jealous seeing the houses and condos that were out of her price range. Even if she tricked and dance double shifts for nights on end, she'd be hard-pressed to live like Storm and Kenya obviously were. Showing her gold teeth, Jordan smiled giving out compliment after compliment. "Wow, you doing the damn thang out here ain't you? You out here living like the white folks live."

Storm laughed having her pull up in the driveway. "I'm straight I guess. But good looking."

"Hey, Storm, I don't know if you still have my number, but here it is in case you need a ride back to the hospital. You know me, you, O.T., and Paris go way back, so don't be a stranger! I'm around anytime, night or day."

Taking the card, Storm glanced at O.T.'s car, which was still parked in the same spot as the night before. "Yo, it ain't gonna be too much longer before the club is reopened. I hope you can come back and still hang with us. I'll squash that bullshit between you and Kenya. She was set tripping anyhow; you good!"

"Don't be silly." Jordan licked her lips seductively as if Storm were a potential trick. "You know I'ma be down with you no matter what. I was there the day you and Deacon first opened the doors and gonna be there when you open that son of a bitch again!"

As Storm headed up the walkway, Jordan backed out of the driveway calling her older sister. "Hey, girlie, thanks for the 411 on my people."

"It wasn't meant to be gossip; it was meant to show you what can happen when you run in those dangerous circles you so intent on running in. That lifestyle can only end up in two ways: dead or in jail!" Nurse Jamison hung up on her always nosey, always street-scheming sibling and tried to get some rest before her next shift started.

Fuck what her goody-goody butt talking about. And Kenya's fake wannabe-boss behind wasn't down there with her man fine ass at all. It's definitely trouble in paradise, and if Kenya don't want him, I showl in the fuck do! If she know like I know, she better bring it because the game is on and payback is a bitch!

Jordan smirked, knowing it wasn't a coincidence that she ran into Storm in front of the hospital when she did. For months she wanted nothing more than to repay Kenya for going in extra hard and embarrassing her in the dressing room of Alley Cats. Now she had the perfect opportunity at hand. Fucking around with Marco Meriwether from time to time, Jordan was grimy and backstabbing. Spoon-feeding him information about Kenya and Storm, who didn't stand up for her that night his girl bugged out, had just hit a brick wall considering ol' boy was now locked up. Now she'd set her own revenge traps.

STORM
Still believing Kenya was on the other side of the door waiting to hit him over the head with a skillet for the harsh message he left, Storm eased his way inside the condo. With all the lights off and the drapes drawn, it was hard for him to see. Knowing it was well past seven o'clock and the house was so quiet immediately bothered him. Even if Kenya was in one of her "everybody, shut the fuck up" moods, London would at least be downstairs watching television or reading.

"Kenya! Yo, Kenya!" Taking the steps three at a time, Storm quickly reached the top of the landing. "Where you at?" he shouted, pushing his bedroom door wide open. "Oh, hell naw! Ain't this some shit!"

The shattered glass from a picture of him and Kenya covered the floor, along with different items of clothing thrown every which way. With the room looking like a tornado had struck, Storm ran over to the walk-in closet, which appeared to be ground zero. Standing in the middle looking at all the bare racks and empty hangers, he got caught in his emotions. *No, the fuck she didn't! This don't make no sense!* Over the past few months he and Kenya had gone through some tough and difficult times but she never ever took as much shit as was missing now. Checking the top drawer on the left-hand side of the dresser, Storm discovered her jewelry as well as his was also gone. *I swear to God, this crazy bitch better not have it!* He rushed to the stash spot, coming up empty-handed.

Before even going to check on a pregnant London, Storm dialed Kenya's cell; of course, he was shot to voicemail. "Hey, you can be pissed the fuck off and pout all you want, but I'ma need that bread back! With O.T. down, you stupid bitch, I'ma need every penny to meet this deadline! So get back home and run my shit!"

Storm threw his phone on the bed and went to talk to London to see if she could tell him what jumped off yesterday when his little brother got shot and if Kenya's lunatic ass said anything about where she was going, although he knew nine outta ten times she was probably at Paris's apartment, like always when they beefed. Walking down the hallway, Storm was stunned stupid when he got to London's door and found almost the same scene as in his and Kenya's bedroom. Clothes were thrown everywhere, hangers were tossed around, drawers were left open, and stuff was wrapped in a blanket. Also near the doorway, Storm saw a case of baby formula. The thick plastic was ripped open, and several cans were missing.

Confused and enraged, that's when he really hit the roof. "First of all, how in the hell did them two get back to speaking terms and who do London think she is taking her ass out this house? She about to deliver any day and she got Kenya dragging her across town to Paris's on some temper tantrum bullshit! Both them Detroit hoes is tripping!"

Storm went back into his bedroom to take quick shower, change clothes, and get back down to the hospital. Even though he was in the mood to drive over to Paris's apartment, kick down the door, and smack the cow shit outta Kenya and London both, he knew O.T. needed him.

With the hookup blessing of a lifetime waiting for him at a stash house and a deadline of seven days and counting, this was the worst time ever to be going through all this turmoil.

Dressed but still angry at the world, Storm ran down the stairs and straight out the front door. Never once did he go into the living room where his son was born, let alone the kitchen walk-in freezer where his son's mother's dead body was. Using his set of keys to O.T.'s car, Storm glanced in the rear seat at all the bags of baby items his brother had purchased for his seed. *That nigga is all in.* Right before he drove off his cell phone rang. Hoping it was Kenya returning his call, he answered without looking at the screen. "Yeah, you dumb ass!"

"Hello?" An older man's voice spoke.

"Damn, my bad. Who is this?"

Finding out it was the contractor doing work at Alley Cats, Storm was distracted from his original game plan having to go by his strip club, currently under renovation, before heading back to O.T.'s bedside. When he got there, Storm was even more frustrated when the man informed him someone had to be on the premises with them until five or six o'clock in the evening to sign off on various final inspections from the city and state. Normally Kenya would've had his back, but now calling her and expecting any type of cooperation was out of the question. *Oh, yeah.* Reaching in his wallet, Storm took out two cards: one from the sassy-mouth female from the day before, Anika, and the other from Jordan. Dialing Jordan's number, he was happy when she picked up on the first ring.

"Yes, hello," the always conniving female purred in the phone like she knew it was a man on the other end.

"Hey, J, this is Storm. I know you just dropped me off, but I need you to do me a solid." Informing her detail by detail of what he need her to do when Jordan showed up at the club, Storm practically hugged her to death for her loyalty, even though Kenya had given her the boot. Introducing the full-breasted scantily clothed beauty to the contractor and his people as the new manager of Alley Cats, Storm gave Jordan two one-hundred dollar bills for her trouble before he drove off.

This shit is working out better than a bitch could ever plan, Jordan schemed, tucking the folded currency in her lace bra. *Wherever Kenya is at, the ho slipping!*

Chapter Six

KENYA

It was nighttime again as Kenya crossed the Michigan state line. Having stopped in a Walmart located in a small town off the interstate, she was fortunate enough to buy a car seat for Li'l Stone as well as some more diapers. Finding out O.T. was lying in the hospital fighting for his life was horrible, true enough. But knowing her own sister was dead, probably because of her, was weighing far more heavy on her mental state of mind. Every time her cell rang or she received a text, she was terrified she'd been found out back in Dallas. Each trooper in each state who just so happened to be parked on the side of the road, Kenya felt was positioned there to apprehend her. At her wits' end, fatigued being a new mother to her kidnapped nephew, the Motown-born-and-raised female got a much-needed second wind, reading the green and white WELCOME TO DETROIT sign. Knowing her long, grueling journey was almost over, Kenya cleared all the missed calls from Storm off her phone and called Brother Rasul.

Practically walking around all day with his cell in his hand, he answered right off rip. "Kenya! Where you at now?"

"I'm on Eight Mile, heading your way in about ten minutes." In a vehicle packed with as many of her belongings that could fit, Kenya kept it moving. No matter what crimes she'd committed or what guilt she was carrying with her, she was still glad to be back home in the D. "Are you by yourself, though?" She looked into the rearview mirror at the car seat and who was asleep in it.

"Look, don't worry, sis. She's not here. It's just me," Brother Rasul reassured Kenya automatically, knowing she was referring to Fatima, London's best friend and confidant. "Just come on. I'll be on the porch waiting. It's all good!"

Brother Rasul was confused as to why Kenya was foolish enough to make that type of road trip so spontaneously, but since she was being so close-lipped throughout every brief conversation they'd had throughout the course of the day, he was at a loss. Once or twice, he was tempted to get in touch with Storm and find out from him what was going on, but he opted to hear it straight from Kenya's mouth like he promised her he would.

Having turned off the elaborate security system and the light-sensor motion detectors, Brother Rasul stood guard on his porch with one of his ever-present handguns tucked in his waistband. He was excited, watching the block like a hawk. Ten short minutes later his homegirl for life was pulling into his driveway.

STORM

"Are you sure he's gonna make it?" Standing vigilantly at his baby brother's bedside, Storm quizzed the team of physicians and specialists who were in and out of the dismal room all afternoon and early evening. "All these tubes and shit can't be good."

"He's holding his own, but it's going to be a good forty-eight hours before we can operate once again." The doctor scanned down O.T.'s chart shaking his head. "His is a most difficult case, and we need to get out of the woods before I can be more optimistic."

Attempting to get back in touch with Kenya or at least London was wearing on Storm's last nerve. After hours he wanted to reach out and call Brother Rasul since he was the only person Kenya ever seemed to listen to; however, he knew first of all his loyalty was to Kenya. And secondly, he knew he'd feel that if he couldn't run his own household, how in the hell was he gonna be able to run business with the new connect? Deciding to swing by Paris's later in the night and bring the twins back home, kicking and screaming if he had to, Storm had to get the ball rolling with coming up with the ticket money due in seven days. With O.T. out of commission, his longtime road dawg Boz dead, and best friend Deacon having been out the picture due to Javier's murderous, brutal tactics, Storm needed someone else he could trust to help hold him down.

"Yeah, can I speak to Ponytail?"

"Who is this?"

"This is Storm. Is he there?"

"Yeah, hold on!" the female hissed into the receiver.

After a brief moment of silence and what seemed like a bit of a loud argument in the background, a dog barking, and a child crying, Storm heard his childhood friend pick up. "I got it! You can hang up!" he shouted out to the female who in turn slammed the phone down as hard as she possibly could. "Yeah, hello."

"Ponytail! My goddamn nigga! What it do!"

"Storm, is that you?"

"Yeah, motherfucker, who you think it is, Santa Claus or some gay-ass shit like that? What's good!"

"Yo, what's been up with you?" Ponytail's smile was so big it was if it Storm could see it through the phone. "Long time, no hear."

"Yeah, dude, I've been trying to make moves low-key and stay outta folk way. You know how I do."

"All right, dig that. Well, I'm glad you called. I've been wondering how things been going with you and O.T."

Leaving his brother's hospital room walking down the crowded hallway looking for a little privacy, Storm continued to talk shit. "It don't sound like ya girl is too happy a nigga hit you up!"

"She just know I'm not down with that street life no more, so when you asked for Ponytail instead of Kevin, she straight bugged out. You know how these females can be at that time of the month. But it ain't no thang. I run my household! You know how I get down!"

"No doubt, no doubt!" Storm quickly agreed knowing time was ticking and in less than twenty-four hours another day would have passed, and he still wouldn't have even broken the seal on the uncut package of heroin. "Well, a nigga like me got some good news and some damn bad."

"Oh, yeah? Well, run it."

"Yeah, dude, first the bad: this crazy bull dyke fucked around and tried to take O.T. out the damn game! Hit his ass at least a good five times!"

"What!" Ponytail's voice rang out causing his girl to get even more irritated by the call out of the blue from her man's childhood running buddy. "Oh, hell naw! You lying! O.T.?"

"Yeah, guy, on the humble over some pussy-ass shit, but they think he gonna be good. I'm posted down here at the hospital right fucking now. Nigga got tubes and machines stuck all up in his black ass!"

"Well, sit tight, fam. We gonna kick it when I see you." Finding out exactly what hospital O.T. was in, Ponytail ended the phone conversation, informing Storm he was on his way and he'd hear the good news update when he got there.

Glad his boy was en route, Storm returned to O.T.'s room, but not before trying to reach Kenya once more, leaving another message. "Yo, Kenya, I know y'all camped out at Paris crib and shit, and you call yourself pissed, but don't spend my bread. I'ma need that shit! I ain't playing!"

KENYA
Forgetting all about a sleeping Li'l Stone, she turned the engine off. Slamming the car door behind her, Kenya ran up onto the porch practically collapsing in Brother Rasul's arms. "Oh my God. I made it. I made it!"

Sensing whatever it was she was going through was deeper than he first imagined, Brother Rasul led her inside his house. "Damn, Kenya, what is it? What's wrong?"

Kenya clutched his arm while peeping around the corner of the living room. "Who here with you?"

"I just told you nobody when you called." He raised his eyebrow. "Now sit down and tell me what in the world is going down so hella urgent that you drove cross-country to get here."

"Did Storm call you? Have you talked to him?"

"Kenya!" Brother Rasul stood over her with his hand reassuringly on her left shoulder. "Stop with the twenty questions you taking me through. What jumped off?"

Burying her face in her hands, Kenya started on her sometimes rambling tearful confession. Initially, the part about her having a miscarriage, followed by Storm going behind her back getting life insurance policies and naming London as the beneficiary, didn't get much a response from Brother Rasul. However, when she added the scattered details of hearing gunfire right outside her window and later finding out from Storm that O.T. had been shot, the tall, burly Muslim in faith ex-bouncer had to sit down.

"It all happened so fast! One minute I was coming down the stairs to tell London to leave my house, then bam." Kenya sobbed struggling to catch her breath with each word she spoke. "I swear I just wanted her to leave, that's all!"

Brother Rasul, always wise beyond his years, was confused in the twisted tale Kenya was laying out. "Wait a minute. O.T., Storm's brother, got shot? Is he alive or what?"

"I guess. Well, yeah. That's what Storm told me."

"Wasn't you there? You said it was just outside y'all condo, if I heard that part correctly."

"It was, but I didn't go outside." Kenya wiped her tears with the sleeve of her sweatshirt. "I don't know why, but I didn't."

Brother Rasul paced the living room floor as the story he was hearing got stranger and stranger. "So that made you get in the car and leave your own house? I mean, I'm sorry, sis, but I don't get it."

Kenya then stood up, slightly moving the curtain so she could check on her vehicle where her nephew was sleeping. "I don't know why I did it. I was so mad!"

"Don't start on that again. Mad at what? At who?"

"London and Storm. They pushed me!" She balled up her fist, and her voice took a harsh tone.

"So you left both of them and came back to Detroit, just like that? Storm probably needs you to hold him down; and isn't your sister, no matter how angry you are at her, ready to deliver?"

"Please, you gotta know I didn't mean it! She was my sister!" Now in a panicked, remorseful state, Kenya walked up to Brother Rasul dropping her head in shame.

This time roughly grabbing both her shoulders, he shook Kenya. "What you mean, was? Kenya, sis, where is London?"

"She's back in Dallas, at the condo, in the walk-in freezer."

A weird silence filled the room as he tried to absorb what she'd just said and what she possibly meant. "Kenya, the freezer? What in the hell is you trying to say?"

"I let London die. Then I hid her body in the rear walk-in freezer!" Kenya's lips quivered as she spoke out loud the horrible act she'd committed supposedly in the name of love.

Holding his head with both hands, Brother Rasul couldn't believe what he'd just heard. *Did she just say what I think she said?* Erratically moving about the room, his heart raced. "Kenya, please tell me you lying! Please tell me you didn't!" He walked from one side of the room to the other. "Where is your damn sister? Kenya! Nawwwww!" Stunned in denial, he was hesitant to ask any further questions in fear of what'd she say next.

Hysterical, Kenya fell to her knees screaming for God to help and forgive her. "I'm sorry! I'm sorry!" she shouted having an all-out hyperventilating fit. "Please, please bring her back! Please! Oh, God! Oh, God! I'm sorry! Please!"

Brother Rasul, although still in disbelief, regained his thought process. Going over to Kenya, he leaned down on the floor trying to get her back up on her feet. "Listen, Kenya, listen, please. You gotta tell me what all went down so I can try to make some sense outta this. First, where is Storm? What did he say?" Before Kenya could answer Brother Rasul turned away, shaking his head. "Kenya, she was pregnant. Damn!"

"I know that!" She frowned pointing toward the door. "He's in the car."

Slowly turning back to face Kenya, Brother Rasul thought he might've heard her wrong. "He who? Who's in the car?"

"The baby. He's out there."

"What! You have a baby in the car, out there?" Brother Rasul wasted no time racing to Kenya's vehicle. Flinging the door open, amid the piles of clothes packed in, he saw the car seat holding the still-sleeping innocent newborn. Carefully removing the baby, car seat and all, he took him inside. After setting the car seat on his dining room table and pulling back the blanket, Brother Rasul was overjoyed to find the wavy-haired infant alive. "All praises due to Allah." He chanted that at least the child was spared Kenya's still-unexplained rage that left her twin dead. "Does Storm even know what has happened or what?"

"I don't really know for sure. The last time his lying ass called, he was down at the hospital seeing about his fake brother and leaving me shady messages!" Arrogant in mindset, Kenya started to behave like she was the victim. "He can kiss where the sun don't shine! His brother can too; he didn't like me from jump!"

Brother Rasul stared at the tiny baby, wondering what he was going to do, as well as what he was willing to do, to help Kenya out this time around. Besides being her confidant since day one at Heads Up, he'd killed Swift protecting her, helped arranged her man's release from Javier's island of horrors, and just vouched for Storm getting credit on the strongest package in his city. He did all of that in the spirit of friendship, but Kenya leaving her twin sister, her own flesh and blood, for dead and then kidnapping her baby was over the top, even in the crazed street life they both led.

POLICE

Having gone home to an empty house, Sergeant Kendricks decided to return to Paris's room under the pretense of getting some information. Even though he'd lied to his partner Malloy, he couldn't lie to himself.

There was something about Paris's beauty, even through her obvious illness, that sparked his interest as a man. Her bone structure and slender lines put his ex-wife in his mind when they first met in high school, back before she'd cheated on him getting pregnant by another dude. As the sworn officer of the law sat there, once again in the daze of a teenage crush, his awkward staring soon turned into him fantasizing about "being" with Paris.

The "do you see this bullshit?" nurses on duty for the shift, who were more in Kendricks's age range of dating, whispered among themselves that his over-attentiveness to the youthful patient, was tasteless if nothing else.

Chapter Seven

JORDAN

After a series of taps on the hotel door, Jordan opened it dressed in a hot pink satin and lace negligee. With seven-inch leather heels on, she pranced back across the room making sure her thick, wide ass was shaking. Turning around, Jordan grabbed both breasts pushing them together. "Do you like what you see, daddy?" she licked her lips.

Usually her trick, who came once a week for over a year, would be knocking her to the king-sized bed by now practically begging her for the pussy, but this time was different. Seemingly uninterested, Big Doc B took his time entering their love shack hideaway room he had paid for six months in advance. Taking a seat on the edge of the bed, Doc looked Jordan up and down trying to get an erection. When she placed his hands on her hips and started to move in a circular motion, Doc didn't paw at her like always or start reaching his hands in places they shouldn't be without an invitation. Instead, he sat there, motionless.

"Hold up! Wait a minute, Jordan. I got something on my mind right now."

"Well, it should be this moist motherfucker here." Sliding one of his hands underneath her lace panties, she made his index finger invade her pussy. "You know you want this."

Still nervous about allowing Kenya to suck his dick and the explosive video she'd somehow managed to record was all Doc could focus on for the last twenty-four hours. Getting some head from Jordan was the last thing on his clouded mind. "I'm gonna just lie back for a few, then I'll be good, all right, baby doll?"

With Big Doc B stretched out on his stomach, Jordan, a relentless freak to her heart, climbed on his back giving him an impromptu massage. As she ground her tiny hands into and across his skin, Doc started to relax. "You like that?"

"Yeah." He felt his troubles temporary lifting as her hot box warmed his lower spine.

"Guess what? I'ma be working back at your favorite spot when they open back up."

"What spot? What you talking about?" Doc moaned to her every touch.

"Alley Cats, nigga!"

"What!" Doc, hearing the name of Storm's club, bucked upward almost tossing Jordan off his back and onto the carpeted floor. "Alley Cats?"

Catching her balance before tipping over Jordan laughed at his reaction she mistook for happiness. "Yeah, guy. Alley Cats, silly! Not only am I gonna be back danc- ing at that motherfucker, but Storm made me a manager today."

"A manager? What about Kenya?" He eased over on his back so he could see her facial expression.

"Fuck that uppity, fake-ass East Coast bitch! She ain't running shit! That's Storm's club anyway not hers!"

Doc was a nervous wreck discussing anything to do with Kenya or Storm period. He closed his eyes, and his stomach ached in the pit knowing his life was now in clear danger. "Just the same, didn't Kenya fire you?"

Jordan was feeling herself. Storm needed her to stand in for his so-called cherished Detroit skank twice, and she knew already that was just the beginning. Crawling off the bed, standing to her feet, Jordan smugly smiled. "For real, for real, if Storm gave a damn what that girl had to say, he wouldn't have been all on me earlier! Plus her ass wasn't even down at the hospital."

Big Doc B was stunned hoping Jordan wasn't referring to anything to do with the allegedly abandoned newborn infant he'd treated yesterday. "What hospital? What are you talking about?"

"O.T."

"What about O.T.?" Doc knew Storm's brother was the hotheaded enforcer of the two, so nine outta ten times if Storm found out what jumped off between him and Kenya, O.T. would be the one to snap his neck. "I'm lost." His nerves were working overtime.

"He got shot. Didn't you hear about it?"

"Naw! When did this happen?" Doc leaped to his feet. Part of him was sympathetic because O.T. always looked out for him down at Alley Cats: free drinks, dances, and low-key sex in the Champagne Room. The other part of him was relieved O.T. was temporarily out of commission, especially considering what he'd done with his future sister-in-law, Kenya.

Jordan went over to the minibar pouring herself a shot of Hennessy knowing their sexual escapades were put on hold. "Remember that chick Vanessa who used to dance at Alley Cats, Bare Backs, and Wild Cherry? Her dance name is Cash N Go?"

"Oh, yeah. Oh, yeah. The tall girl with the double Ds." Doc remembered getting one, maybe two "special attention" dances from her.

"Yeah, that's her." Jordan downed the shot as if it were only water. Going to get the entire bottle, she took another shot setting the liquor next to the bed. "Well, it was a thugged-out stud bitch named Tangy who fucks with Vanessa on the regular. I guess ol' girl was mad O.T. was giving her girlie the dick. Bam, she shot him."

"You lying?"

"Naw. Storm said five bullets!"

"Damn. Was she pregnant by chance, the dancer?" Amazed, his eyebrows raised over the chaotic soap opera story she was telling and tried to find out if the dancer she was talking about was the one who had entrusted Kenya with the little baby boy.

Jordan swayed over toward Big Doc B dropping down on her knees. As she tilted her head back, her widened eyes remained focused on his. "Well, I don't know if it went down exactly like that, but word on the street is it did. And pregnant? That gold-digging ho, Cash N Go? I don't think so!"

"And Kenya?" He helped Jordan unzip his pants.

"Yo, I told you fuck Kenya, dude!" She slurped while talking shit. "Apparently she's out the picture, ghost or something! That's why Storm's on me! Shit, when I asked him about her, he was acting all stank even hearing her damn name."

"Kenya, out the picture? You sure? I just saw her earlier." Letting that information slip, Doc moaned having a flashback of the forbidden head he'd been blessed with or cursed with, depending on who found out. Now her bizarre actions made a little more sense. She was beefing with Storm and was just grudge sexing. *Damn, if that was the case I would've hit that all the way.* Doc's freaky one-track mind fantasized, enjoying Jordan suck him off wishing it was Kenya.

"So what if you saw her dumb ass at the mall or whatever? Now you seeing me!" Jordan deep-throated Doc shutting him up from riding Kenya's coattails.

Enjoying an hour or so of over-the-top, raunchy, head-board-banging sex, busting nut after nut up in her pussy raw dog, Doc paid Jordan $400 just as usual, leaving her laid out buck-naked sprawled across the hotel room bed. Seconds after Doc left, Jordan's cell rang. Storm. She grinned as his name flashed on her screen and started blinking repeatedly.

STORM

Storm met Ponytail at the front entrance of the hospital. After taking him up to briefly visit his brother, Storm and he went three floors down to the hospital chapel for some privacy. As they knelt at a small altar, Ponytail listened to his old friend's dilemma and what he wanted or more like needed him to do.

"My girl is gonna bug out. I promised her I was done with all this bullshit after she had the second baby."

"I know, man, but this thang with O.T. got me all the way fucked up. I need somebody I can trust. Somebody who ain't gonna rob me blind, ya feel me?"

Ponytail rubbed his perfectly lined beard trying to find a way to help Storm that didn't involve him getting back into the game. "I know where you coming from, fam, but what about all your street soldiers you had riding with you? Ain't none of them ready for a bump?"

"Dude, since some trouble we had with that old ancient motherfucker Royce and his damn lieutenant Marco, shit been real shady around the way trying to keep some stand-up niggas on the team. Most of 'em is straight faggots and shit." Storm was getting loud and had to tone the volume of his voice down. "But now both them problems is out the way, I'm 'bout to rebuild. That's why I need you, man! With my brother on his back, it ain't no other guy alive I trust with my life, my wife, and my package but you!"

Desperately behind on his bills and fighting a fore-closure on his house, Ponytail weighed the options. "All right, Storm, but just until O.T. ass is back on his feet!"

"All right, that's a bet!" Storm gave him a pound. "Welcome back, my nigga! Welcome motherfucking back!"

When Ponytail left heading home to break the news to his girl of his plans to start slinging again, Storm stopped back in to check on his brother one last time before leaving for the night. Seeing O.T. was stabilized and all was as good as could be expected, he left him in Nurse Jamison's compassionate care. Before starting his engine, Storm tried calling Kenya then London. Still no response. He headed over to Paris and O.T.'s apartment.

Driving into the parking lot, his eyes searched the area for any signs of Kenya's car. *Knowing her, she probably parked the bitch around the corner or some old, sneaky shit like that.* With each step he took, Storm grew angrier he had to go through all of this to just get his girl and baby momma to be back under his roof. *Whoever said pimping ain't easy told the damn truth!* Pressing his ear against the door to see if he heard the sisters talking or maybe the sounds of the television, Storm was met with dead silence. Using his set of keys, he slowly opened the door to the dark, seemingly deserted unit. *Ain't this a bitch! Where is them hoes?* Storm hit the light switch in each room throughout the apartment seeing no indica-tion that Kenya or London had even been there. The back of each television felt cold, and every dish in the kitchen was untouched.

"Where in the fuck is they at?" Storm yelled taking his phone off his hip calling London and getting her voicemail, then Kenya. "Yeah, you crazy bitch, I'm over your girl house! Since you and your sister think this shit is a joke, let's see who gonna be laughing when I catch up with y'all asses! You got London out there pregnant like this is funny." He was boiling with fury, and in the midst of his rage he stepped right over a small scalpel on the bedroom floor belonging to his buddy, Big Doc B. "What you trying to do, make her lose the baby 'cause you can't have none?" Hanging up his cell, Storm once again knew he'd gone too far saying what he'd just said, but Kenya was trying his patience all the way around.

Going into the bathroom to take a leak, something strange caught his eye. "Oh, hell naw, they asses was here. Slick bitches!" Touching a balled-up washcloth on the sink that was still damp in the middle was a dead giveaway someone had been there not too long ago. Figuring they probably ducked out and gone to a hotel when he had called earlier telling Kenya he knew where she was, Storm calmed down and left.

Stopping by Wendy's to grab a combo meal, Storm was exhausted when he got back home. Darting straight up the stairs without bothering to turn on any lights or check the mail, Storm wolfed down his food, jumped into a hot shower, then fell back across the bed with the towel wrapped around his lower body. *Damn, I almost forgot!* Reaching for his phone, he dialed Jordan's number to get an update on what went down at Alley Cats.

POLICE

"Well, damn, it's about time you came into the station to make your reports. I was starting to think you took a vacation and forgot to tell me," Malloy joked as his partner came in to start the 6:00 a.m. shift.

Kendricks was still somewhat distracted from his multiple visits to Paris, which he cloaked with waiting for her to speak, and they had the best of him. "I know, but since the shooting of one of the Christian brothers, we need every lead we can get to build a strong case on the other one."

"I know. That's why I'm having that fool Marco Meriwether brought up here from lockup. We know he killed
that mother at the ATM and the young guy he was staying with, but I'm gonna see what he has to say about his
old buddy, the late, great, wanted-to-be Shaft Royce,
and the drug war between him and his cross-town rival,
Storm. Hell, the ballistics match on the slugs taken out
of Storm's bodyguard, Boz, and the Robinson kid!"

Kendricks continued to scroll through his cell looking
at pictures he'd taken of an IV-induced sleeping Paris.
"Yeah, he's already looking at life, if not the death penalty.
Right about now he might be looking to turn over on the
next man." He hardly looked away from the screen as he
spoke.

"Yeah, Kendricks, that's what I'm hoping." Malloy
poured a cup of freshly brewed coffee. Shaking his
head, he peered out the window into the busy parking
lot. "In between dealing with that crazy fuck Marco, a
fact-finding visit from one of the damn goody-goody city
council members, and the invasions of students on a field
trip, shit around here gonna be real hectic."

Thirty-five minutes later, a uniformed officer was
coming through the door arguing with prisoner Marco
Meriwether. "Didn't I say shut up?"

"Man, fuck you!" Marco hissed struggling to break
free of the tight handcuffs. "If I didn't have these sons of
bitches on, I'd fuck your cornball ass up!"

"Whatever." The rookie shoved Marco down to the
wood bench in the corner of the homicide squad room.
"Is this where y'all want this animal?"

"Yeah, that's good." Malloy put on his game face as
he approached Marco. He and Kendricks had already
determined he was gonna play the role of the bad cop
and his partner, who was slightly younger, the good. "Mr.
Meriwether!"

Marco frowned as they locked eyes. Even though he was young in age, he was far from being a newcomer to the law. Having been in and out of juvenile facilities since he was eleven, Marco was prepared for the cat-and-mouse game that was about to jump off. "Yeah, nigga, that's right. So what's the deal? You playing the black hat or the white?"

"Look here, you piece of dog shit, your boy O.T. Christian is in the hospital clinging to life and the way his brother was talking maybe I should give him a minute alone with you!"

"Oh, you black hat in this motherfucker!" Marco cracked a smile letting Malloy know he peeped him out. "Fuck that fag O.T. being shot! I didn't do the shit! And real rap, fuck that buster Storm, too! I ain't fearing no nigga!"

"Is that right, big man?" With a vein jumping in his neck, Malloy grew more agitated by the moment. "You ain't scared of that death penalty you looking at? You that hard?"

"Look, here's an idea. Why don't you send ya boy in the white hat to get me a Pepsi or a Mountain Dew while you act tough? By the time he get back, I'll talk shit to him. Then both y'all fucks can argue over who gonna escort me back to my cell! Is that a plan or what?"

Snatching him up by the collar, Malloy gave Marco what he wanted: the roughhouse treatment. "Listen, boy," he hissed with his hot coffee breath in his face, "okay, you think you know the game, but did you anticipate this part?" Slamming his fist into Marco's stomach, Malloy let him drop down to the bench.

"You ho-ass motherfucker," Marco, still handcuffed, gasped looking up with contempt. "I'll kill you and your family!"

Kendricks leaped to his feet running over toward his partner and grabbing his arm. "Malloy, just chill out."

"Oh, the game done started, huh?" Marco's cuffs dug deeper into his wrist as he moved around. "That was quick!"

Luckily before any more police brutality could take place against Marco, Malloy was called out of the office to conduct a guided tour with the junior high students who'd just arrived and then he had to participate in a brief mandatory presentation about careers in law enforcement.

"So it's like that, huh?" Marco sat straight up. "Ya manz gonna sucker punch me in the gut and you gonna let these cuffs cut off my circulation? That shit foul as a motherfucker!"

Getting a call from the doctor in charge of Paris's care, Kendricks had no time for Marco's mouth. "Be quiet, dude!"

"Yo, yo! These cuffs is killing me, man!" Marco ignored Kendricks's pleas to take it down a notch. "I can't feel my damn hands and shit! Yo! I'm serious! Damn white hat! Yo!"

Not being able to hear what the doctor was saying, Kendricks asked him to hold the line. Having had enough of Marco's boisterous complaints, Kendricks went over loosening the handcuffs on each hand. "Are you happy? Now shut your fucking mouth!"

With his back turned, Kendricks sat at his desk returning to his call with the doctor. Deep into the conversation, the trained officer of the law didn't pay attention to the fact he hadn't heard the click of one of the steel restraints when he did Marco that favor to keep him silent. Maneuvering his right hand out the cuff, Marco stood to his feet. One cuff dangling, slowly, he crept up on Kendricks from behind. Lifting an industrial-size stapler off one of the desk he slammed it down across the rear of the sergeant's skull. No sooner than Kendricks's limp body hit the ground, a puddle of blood gushed out of the gash. Using the officer's keys, he unfastened the other cuff then smiled. Taking the sergeant's gun and cell phone, Marco looked at the office door, knowing that trying to get out that way was an immediate death sentence waiting to happen.

Bolting over to the window, and climbing out of the one-story dwelling was an easy alternative. Still dressed in street clothes, but no laces in his sneakers, Marco dashed into the parking lot just as a car was pulling in. Sticking Kendricks's police-issued firearm inside the open window of the vehicle, he shoved the muzzle to the side of the driver's head. "Yo, hit the locks, motherfucker, and let me in before I put some of these hot ones up in you," he loudly demanded snatching the suit-wearing city councilman out of the dark four-door sedan.

As Marco drove off into the early morning traffic, he could hear the stunned carjacking victim yelling for help.

Chapter Eight

STORM

Feeling the vibration of his cell phone on the bed, a still-towel-clad Storm woke up. At seven o'clock, with eyes still half shut, he realized how exhausted he must've been. In between dealing with O.T. being hurt, Kenya acting a fool, London running around pregnant, and meeting the connect his mind was jumbled. The last thing Storm remembered doing was talking to Jordan about the renovations at Alley Cats. Before he could get up to take an early morning piss his cell was vibrating again. Reaching over he pushed the side button lighting up the screen. "Damn, I know, I know," he mumbled seeing the number 6.

Standing up, leaving the towel on the bed, a naked Storm walked into the bathroom. Deciding to take another shower to wake himself up, he adjusted the water temperature. Five minutes into the hot, streaming water from the nozzle pouring on top of his head, he was interrupted by the sound of a horn blowing in his driveway. Looking out the small window, he rubbed the moisture off. He couldn't help but laugh at the one-of-a-kind vehicle. Throwing on a pair of track pants and a wife beater, Storm jogged down the stairs opening the front door. "What you doing here so early? It's like seven, seven-thirty. Your ass must be ready to put in work for real."

Ponytail unlocked his rear hatch of his customized station wagon taking out a huge duffle bag. Talking over the sounds of his albino pit bull, Reckless, barking in the rear seat, he explained his situation. "Dude, I told you my girl wasn't gonna go for that 'I'm only gonna slang for a minute' bullshit. Shit, ten minutes of me coming into the crib she was on my back. By the time she finish going off, I was tired as a fuck." Ponytail let Reckless outside of the car putting on his leash. "When a nigga woke up, my bag was already packed. She told me and him to get to stepping!"

"Hell naw!" Storm protested feeling like he'd broken up a happy home asking his boy to help him out.

"It's all good, guy. I needed a vacation anyway." He spit on the grass while trying to control the loud, vicious dog that was trying to break free. "So now we gotta post up here. Ya girl ain't gonna care is she?"

Storm looked back at the empty condo and shrugged his shoulders. "Even if she did, ya ass is family to me."

Making sure Ponytail had a strong grip on Reckless, Storm led them both inside the house. Believing London would be back in a few days after Kenya cooled off, he didn't want Ponytail sleeping in her room, if only temporarily. Since the basement was remodeled, he took him downstairs telling him he could stay as long as he wanted to. Not comfortable with the dog, aka Cujo, who was less than friendly, running loose in the crib, Storm gave his longtime homeboy two options: one, he'd gladly pay for a kennel to board the animal; or two, he could stay in the huge empty storage room separating the kitchen and the walk-in freezer.

"Yo, he a straight-up nutcase!"

"I feel you, Storm. He just ain't that good with strangers, but my kids love him." Choosing the second option, Ponytail grabbed the still-barking four-legged growling menace by the collar. "Come on, Reckless. Come on, boy."

Standing on the other side of the large kitchen, Storm was cautious, to say the least. He let them both pass, wishing he had his gun just in case the strong-willed beast broke away from Ponytail's grip. Only a few yards from the walk-in freezer, which was now secretly a temporary tomb for London and the dreadful truth, he shook his head. Storm made up in his mind right then and there he wasn't going anywhere near that direction unless absolutely necessary. Amused, the pair of them stood back watching Reckless scratch wildly on the freezer door and sniff at the bottom. Storm and Ponytail chalked it up to the dog being hungry and obviously smelling food on the other side, certainly not a corpse.

Leaving his friend to get settled, Storm went back upstairs to get dressed. Slipping his belt through the loops, he stopped when his cell rang. "Yeah? Hey, Jordan."

"You fell asleep on me last night."

"I know. I was out my mind. I woke up with the towel still on from my shower."

"Wow, that sounds interesting as hell," Jordan flirted while still trying to be slick. "I know Kenya was happy."

Changing the subject after hearing Kenya's name, Storm cut to the chase. "So do I remember you telling me you got all the final inspection paperwork?"

Sensing she'd struck a nerve by his tone, Jordan smirked. "Yeah, Storm baby, you know I got you covered. I have the papers right here on the nightstand. You want me to drop them off or do you wanna meet me for breakfast?"

Storm had a lot on his plate and decided to kill two birds with one stone. "Listen, J, do me a favor and run them by the hospital. I'll be there about noon."

"Okay, babe. And, listen, the contractor said—"

"Hold tight, J. I got another call coming in from a strange number. Matter of fact I'll hit you back in a few."

Storm ended that conversation by clicking over to the other line. "Yeah, hello."

"Bitch-made nigga!"

"What!"

"You heard me! Bitch-ass-made nigga! So ya little brother got hit, huh?"

"Who in the fuck is this?' Storm looked at the number not recognizing it.

"Who you think faggot?"

Having had enough of entertaining the caller's bullshit, Storm hung up. Two seconds later his cell was ringing again. It was the same number. "Yo, whoever the fuck this is, ya best bet is to stop calling this motherfucker!"

Avoiding several cars by flashing his lights and blowing the horn, Marco came up on his exit. "Damn, Storm, you should know better by now not to threaten ol' Marco. I don't like that kinda shit. Real rap it could get you like that ho-ass brother of yours: shot the fuck up!"

Storm was confused. Less than twenty-four hours ago, Detective Malloy was at the hospital claiming Marco was locked up; now he was calling his cell phone going hard like it wasn't shit. "Let me tell you something, nigga—"

"Naw, let me tell you," Marco cut him off while pulling into a hotel parking lot. "The game is back on, and since your brother is on an indefinite timeout, after I kill you, I'ma do that pregnant bitch of yours in his place!"

Storm was furious as he snatched up the remote. Turning on the television to see breaking news on every channel about Marco Meriwether's daring escape from police headquarters in broad daylight, his assault on an officer, and the carjacking of a city councilman, he cringed. "If your punk ass is that brazen to think you can fuck with me and mines, nigga, come on down, ya feel me?"

"Don't worry, dude, I got you. Be patient." He surveyed his surroundings. "In due time you and ya brother gonna be laid the fuck out just like ya manz Boz was!"

Suddenly ending the call, Marco found what he was searching for in the semi-crowded parking lot. *I thought so.* Driving off the premises, he abandoned the stolen sedan eight blocks over on a residential street knowing it was probably now being tracked by GPS. Throwing Sergeant Kendricks's cell phone against a concrete wall for the same high tech reasons, he quickly hiked it back to the hotel.

Inconspicuous as possible, Marco walked through the lobby taking the elevator up to the fifth floor. When he got to room 521, he checked to make sure the coast was clear. Wasting no more time, he removed Sergeant Kendricks's gun from the rear of his waistband. As his heart raced, his adrenalin rose and his dick got hard. Rubbing his recently bald head, Marco missed his thick dreadlocks as he knocked twice on the fifth-floor door.

"Who is it?" the voice from the other side asked.

Avoiding the security peephole, Marco stood over to the side of the door sinisterly replying, "Room service."

JORDAN

Content hearing Storm's smooth voice, Jordan slid her thong to the side and fingered herself imaging it was him bringing her so much pleasure. When he'd fallen asleep on her the night before, she stayed on the line listening to him breathe for at least twenty minutes before hanging up. The fact that he called her almost the first thing this morning was getting her hotter by the second. Trying to get Storm to go to breakfast or maybe meet her over at her apartment didn't seem to be working out. He claimed he had other shit to do.

With two fingers now soaking wet in her snatch, Jordan tried to find out where Kenya was so early, but Storm wasn't falling for that either. *This motherfucker is playing hardball with my pretty ass, I see.* She was on the verge of cumming from just listening to his rough-boy swag tone when his other end rang interrupting her flow. "And, listen, the contractor said—" Not satisfied the evening before by her and Big Doc B's sexual exploits nor the fat, stank-ass city inspector she let fuck her brains out behind the bar to ensure Storm got his final paperwork, Jordan was hoping Storm would take up the slack. "Damn, ain't that a bitch!" she fumed after he abruptly ended the conversation getting another call and telling her to meet him at the hospital. "It don't matter how hard his ass act, he gonna be mine!"

Having had smoked half a blunt of Kush, Jordan kept on her mission to cum for the second time, when out of the blue someone knocked on the door. *Who in the fuck?* She climbed out of the bed going over to the door. "Who is it?"

When the man on the other side answered, "Room service," immediately she shook her head thinking Big Doc B must've called in a breakfast order for her.

"Just a minute," Jordan put on her silk robe thinking how sweet Doc's good-tricking behind truly was.

STORM

Shit, this ugly motherfucker got more lives than a goddamn cat! Storm folded his arms as he switched from channel to channel seeing Marco's mug shot flash repeatedly. Without them dreads dangling in his face he look like *Helter Skelter* or some crazy bullshit like that. Not believing his bad luck, he ran over to the closet, which was still in shambles, and he got another one of his guns. "If this nigga wanna meet the devil so bad, I'ma send him on his damn way," Storm snarled loading both clips.

Wringing together both his sweaty hands, he prayed Kenya would stop playing the "I'm pissed at you" game and bring her black ass home. It was one thing when he thought Marco was locked up in jail, but now the savage was back out roaming the streets, looking for nothing better to do but terrorize him and his. Pushing her number up, he waited. One ring, two rings, three rings. *Fucking voicemail again!* Trying London's cell, he got the same reaction. Logging on to Facebook, he saw Kenya hadn't posted in the last few days either. *I hope they dumb asses is watching the damn news!* Knowing the shit he was dealing with had gone from bad to worse, Storm finally broke down. Scrolling through his contacts, he came to the Bs. "I hope this guy done heard from her or maybe London talked to his girl." Turning away from the television, he was elated while at the same time ashamed when Brother Rasul answered.

"*As sala'amu alaikum.*"

"*Walaikum as sala'am,*" out of respect Storm replied. "Hey there, good brother, I hate to bother you, especially since you already done looked out so swell."

Brother Rasul was on edge but played it cool. He knew sooner or later Storm would get around to calling him if he hadn't heard from Kenya or worse than that discovered London's dead body. Having not really got the entire uncut version of what went down to prompt Kenya to blink out and do what she'd done, he was at a total disadvantage over what exactly to say or not say. "So I guess that situation worked out for you, huh? I haven't heard from my people so—"

"Yeah, yeah, that was super tight," Storm fired back with gratitude. "I'ma be all right for sure. But, I don't know if you heard or not, but my brother took a few hot ones."

"Damn, is he good?"

"Yeah, he's holding his own. O.T. is too strong to check out this piece without a fight!"

"That's a blessing." Trying to be sympathetic but at the same time rush him off the line before he started talking about Kenya didn't work. "I'ma pray for your family. Y'all stay strong and take care."

"Wait, wait, hold up," Storm protested. "I know this is gonna sound kinda crazy and all but . . ."

Brother Rasul had just put into his car the last of the bags he'd just purchased from Kmart for Storm's newborn son who was back at his house sleeping. He could tell that, at least, Storm hadn't found London at this point, because if he did, he wouldn't have been as semi-calm as he was. "Yeah, what up, doe?"

These Detroit niggas with this "what up, doe" bullshit, Storm said to himself before asking the million dollar question. "I know this question is out the blue, but have you spoken to my girl in the last day or so?"

"Kenya?" he stupidly replied wasting time as he sat behind the steering wheel yet to start the engine. "Well, to be honest—"

Getting a burning gut feeling that maybe he had, Storm interjected. "Listen, man, I'm not trying to put you in the middle, but that nutcase-ass motherfucker who was giving me and my brother so much trouble, Marco Meriwether, he done broke the hell outta lockup, ya feel me? Then dawg had the nerve to call my cell talking cash shit! So if you talked to Kenya or Fatima done talked to London let me know."

Realizing at this point Kenya's fiancé obviously hadn't been in the walk-in freezer to discover his dead baby momma, Brother Rasul chose his words carefully. "Well, I did speak to Kenya, and she was kinda confused."

"Brother Rasul, I'ma keep it a hundred. I said some pretty fucked-up shit to her, but she just bugged out for no good reason. Now she's hiding out in some hotel somewhere, with London's naïve pregnant ass following right behind her," Storm explained as he glanced behind him to see Marco's breaking news escape update flash across the flat screen. "I really wasn't tripping at the fact that she hasn't been answering my calls, but with ol' boy out and about, I don't want her and London getting caught in the crossfire on the humble."

At a loss for words, Brother Rasul paused. "Okay, I tell you what. Let me handle some business first, and then I'll try to talk to Kenya and see what's what. That's the best I can do, brother, and I'll definitely tell her about Marco."

Ending it like that, Storm went downstairs to put Ponytail up on the latest 411.

KENYA/ BROTHER RASUL

Just back in from Kmart buying a small bassinet and a few other items needed for the newborn, Brother Rasul found Kenya still fast asleep in the middle of the bed he and Fatima shared when she was home from the university. At thirty-six years old, he had seen and dealt with plenty of women in his lifetime. However, even thinking back to the first time he met Kenya inside of Heads Up, he knew there was something special about her. Taking in account both she and Fatima were about sixteen or seventeen years his junior, he thought it was their youthful approach to the world that made him so mentally held captive.

Having just heard what Storm had told him, he was torn. Trying to fight the feeling of his manhood rise, Brother Rasul stared at every curve on Kenya. *I know this ain't right*. His eyes traced her body as his mind pulled back the burgundy satin sheet. *Down boy!* he demanded watching her squirm as she woke up. *Down!*

"Oh, hey." Kenya sat up in the bed wearing only a T-shirt belonging to Fatima. "What time is it?" She yawned rubbing her weary eyes.

Brother Rasul tried his best to hide his hard-on, hoping not to embarrass himself or disrespect their solid friendship. "It's going on noon."

"Oh, my God, the baby!" Kenya jumped out the bed forgetting she had just a T-shirt and a pair of pink panties on. "He needs to eat!"

Allah, please forgive me. His dick saluted once again. "Don't worry, li'l sis. I fed and changed li'l man before I went to Kmart. He's 'sleep right there." Brother Rasul pointed to the huge dresser drawer he temporary cleaned out.

"Kmart? Dang, I've been knocked out that long?" Kenya reached back pulling the sheet off the bed and wrapping herself in it.

"I knew you needed to rest. After what you told me last night, I know you couldn't have been thinking to clearly. I figured after a good night's rest, some hot food in your stomach, and a shower you could tell me what really went down."

Not wanting to relive what was the worst day of her life, Kenya stalled. "But I already—"

"Kenya, we done been through a lot, so don't ask me to try to help you if you ain't ready to keep it real okay?"

"Yes." She nodded indicating he was correct.

"Now here's a towel and a washcloth. *Mi casa es su casa.*" He tossed them to her from across the room. "Okay, I'll be downstairs waiting. We need to talk for real, truthful, and up front, especially since I just lied to Storm."

With her body trembling, Kenya headed toward the shower still wrapped in the sheet. Allowing it to fall to the marble floor, she stepped into the glass-enclosed stall.

Lost in the pulsating, steaming hot water, she knew when she got out all hell was probably going to break loose. *Damn, I know Storm done told Ra I just let London die.* She sobbed closing her eyes wishing she could turn back the hands of time. *And I sucked Doc's dick. What have I done? My whole life is so fucked up!*

Chapter Nine

POLICE

Rushed through the same emergency room as O.T. had been days before, Police Sergeant Kendricks was still semiconscious reeling from the massive blow he'd suffered at the hands of the deranged killer Marco Meriwether. Hallucinating as the doctors examined the clotting injury on the rear of his head, they discovered it was worse than they originally thought. Using several packages of gauze to soak up the excess amount of blood matted in his hair, the nurse did what she could do to keep her patient as calm as possible.

"What caused this size gash?" The doctor put on surgical gloves before probing his finger along the sides of the open wound. "It's extremely deep."

Detective Malloy was infuriated with his partner, recently distracted from his job, while still concerned for his well-being. Standing over to the side, he finally answered the question, "Yeah, we believe it was a desk stapler. It was found on the floor next to him."

"A stapler?" the doctor quizzed seeing the depth of the hole.

"It was a pretty big one, office size, real heavy-like."

"Oh, I see." He raised his eyebrow. "Okay, everybody out, we need to run a few tests."

Checking in with the chief commander of the task force apprehension unit, Malloy paced the floor wondering just what in the hell went down in his and Kendrick's office that gave handcuffed Marco Meriwether the chance to attack his valued colleague, not to mention escape. "None of this bullshit makes any sense," he shouted into the phone before he got chewed out from the chief.

"Look here, Malloy, shit happens, but not no bullshit like this. We all put in a lot of overtime manpower hours to lock that lunatic up in the first place. Now you and your man is gonna take the heat for this one." He swore as his other lines flashed indicating a flood of other incoming calls. "That damn city councilman he jacked and the fucking mayor been on the television all morning questioning the entire department's competence!"

Confused at the circumstances himself, Malloy could only lower his head. "I don't know what to tell you, sir. He was locked up when I left."

"At this point, it don't matter what happened when you left! It's on both y'all, you and Kendricks!" the chief, frustrated in attitude, angrily fired back. "Now if you're finished over there holding your partner's hand, I'd suggest you get over here and suit up with the rest of the men and hit the streets. Until that fool Marco, whatever the fuck his name is, is recaptured, ain't nobody on this goddamned force resting, especially you!"

MARCO

Staring down at the knob turn, Marco readied himself for what he might find on the other side of the door. Knowing Jordan and her whorish ways like he did, there was no telling what guy or girl she had spent the night freaking with, so he had to be prepared.

"I didn't order any room service." Jordan smiled while naïvely opening the door slightly.

Using his strength, Marco slammed his free hand on the wood knocking an unsuspecting Jordan to the floor.

Rushing inside with his gun pointed ready to fire if need be, Marco pushed the door shut behind him. "Who the hell else in this motherfucker with you?" he demanded as his eyes peered at the bathroom threshold and his nostrils flared. "Who fucking else?"

Jordan couldn't move. She couldn't speak. It was as if she were looking at a ghost. In between talking to Storm and masturbating she hadn't bothered to turn on the news to worry herself with the outside business of the world. If she had, she would've been possibly prepared for Marco's gun being pointed at her. Hearing him ask her once more if she was alone, Jordan finally found the courage to speak. Swallowing a lump in her throat, the words came out. "Ain't nobody here, Marco." She trembled scared of what he was gonna do next. "I thought you—"

Marco headed toward the bathroom to double-check for himself. "Yeah, I know you did." He knew what she was about to say. "The ho-ass police can't hold me the fuck down."

As if she were waiting for permission to move, Jordan stayed down on the floor. "Well—"

"Well, my motherfucking ass, bitch! Even before them punks knocked me, you had been fell off dealing with me. When my money got low and ran out, so did you!"

When he lowered his gun, she felt it was okay to at least get up and sit on the edge of the bed. "Marco, I swear to God it wasn't nothing personal." Jordan held her robe tightly closed acting like she and Marco hadn't been fuck buddies for months back when he was still making money with Royce. "It's just that—"

Marco laid the pistol down on the dresser knowing Jordan wasn't foolish enough to make a play for it. Just hours ago, he believed he wouldn't have the pleasure of female companionship for the rest of his life. Now,

Marco grabbed at his dick. Roughly shoving one of his hands underneath Jordan's silk robe, he felt up her breasts. Sensing she wasn't feeling his advances, Marco got caught in his emotions. Yoking her up, his hand tightened around her neck. "Bitch, I know you ain't tripping is you?"

Seeing the look of fury, revenge, and murder in his face, Jordan quickly decided it would be in her best interest to play along. "It's not that, Marco. I just was wondering how you got out so soon that's all." She struggled to speak.

"Later for all that; first give me some of that fat cat of yours."

"Wait a minute, Marco, okay?" Jordan wanted to get a drink to settle her nerves first.

"For what? I know you don't think I'm about to pay for this tore-up motherfucker no more!" He rammed his hand in between her legs sticking two fingers inside of her.

Wanting to jump up and smack the shit out of him for talking to her like that, especially without paying for the privilege, Jordan knew he was desperate and had no problem whatsoever adding her to his ever-growing list of victims. "I just wanted to take a shot that's all." Still terrified, she nodded her head over to the nightstand where a bottle of liquor was sitting.

Marco stopped violating her innards long enough to see his three most favorite things in the world after pussy within arm's reach: money, Hennessy, and a blunt. "Damn you ballin'! You up in this bitch partying like a motherfucker ain't you!" First snatching up the $400 Big Doc B had left for Jordan, stuffing it in his pants pocket, Marco laughed. Twisting the cap off the bottle, he then took the dark demon to the head. Shaking his shoulders after the stiff morning eye-opener, he reached for the half-smoked blunt that was resting on a manila envelope, firing it up. "Now this is what I'm talking about!" Inhaling two good times, he noticed the name ALLEY CATS written across the envelope. *What the fuck?* he thought as he choked on the strong weed. Picking it up, he held the blunt in between his lips as he opened the packet. "Yo, what you doing with some shit that say Alley Cats on it?"

As he glanced over the notarized papers, Jordan could see him getting aggravated. She knew his beef with both Storm and O.T. was still very much on. "Well, um, Storm kinda made me the new club manager." She stuttered out of fear that she was now dealing with the guy they both claimed to have hated. "And when it reopens it's gonna be a lot of money flowing through that spot and my bills—"

"Bills?" Marco nonchalantly tossed the documents to the carpeted floor. "Bitch, please; sell your pussy or some of that good head of yours like you always do! If nobody else tearing you off, I know that doctor buster is!"

"Whatever." Jordan's normal reaction would be to tell the average nigga to go fuck himself then die in his sleep, but she knew Marco Meriwether's project-raised ass was far from average. Saying anything remotely smart would undoubtedly get her beat down. *I wish I could call Storm right now to get at this cocky fool!*

Turning on the television, Marco grinned with sheer satisfaction watching pictures and news reports about him on almost every channel. "Look at the mayor's faggot ass talking that shit! Ahhh naw, that crybaby buster was a councilman!" Elated he was such a "hood celebrity" he soon unfastened his pants letting them drop to his ankles. Falling back on the king-sized unmade bed like he was a true boss and not a cold-blooded fugitive, Marco gave Jordan one more command before he hit the blunt again. "Bitch, get over here and suck my dick and don't make me ask you twice!"

Minutes into the free blowjob, he made a statement sending chills throughout Jordan's entire body. "Alley Cats ain't never gonna reopen and if it do your boy Storm ain't gonna live to see it! That's my word! Now keep at it and make this bad boy throw up!"

STORM

After relocating the shipment to a safe stash closer to his dope houses that were still fortunate enough to still be up and slinging, especially considering the full court press of the police and the murderous reign of terror Marco was putting down on the Christian Brothers, Storm and Ponytail sat down going over a careful game plan for citywide distribution. Introducing his old running buddy and new right-hand man to his few loyal street soldiers, Storm warned those of them who didn't know that despite earlier information that Marco had been knocked, that info was now irrelevant because he'd escaped and was back on the street.

"Watch y'all back. Until we get a chance to catch that motherfucker, we gotta be on alert," Storm strongly advised while cracking his knuckles. "He better hope the cops catch back up with his ass before I do, because at least they'll let the lunatic live!"

Leaving Ponytail and his crew to figure out the details, Storm left to go check on his brother's condition along with meet up with Jordan. Getting in line at the crowded valet parking driveway, he texted Jordan informing her he'd just pulled up at the hospital and for her to call whenever she arrived. As luck would have it seconds after stepping foot inside the hospital lobby, Storm ran into none other than Detective Malloy.

"Well, I'll be damned, not you the fuck again!" Storm was not in the mood for any more interrogations or word games, and it showed. "Is you following me or what?"

Malloy, who was also not in the mood for the bullshit, especially after just having been chewed out by his commander, took a deep breath before responding. "Look, despite what you and your brother may think the entire police department wasn't designed to keep tabs on you two. I'm here on other business."

"Please don't tell me your partner is the one who let ol' boy break camp. Tsk, tsk, tsk. Y'all some clowns for real! Anyway, from what's been all over the news, shouldn't you be out trying to play super cop?"

"Don't tell me how to do my job, you slimeball thug. If it weren't for lowlifes like you and Marco the world would be perfect."

Storm took a few steps back and laughed. "Awww, ain't that some shit? If I didn't have to check on my brother, I'd stay here all day and play with your nine to five ass, but . . ."

Heading toward the door, Malloy finally cracked a smile giving Storm something to think about. "Maybe we'll take our time apprehending Marco Meriwether. That way he can finish the job that dyke started. When we were dragging him off that bus, the only thing he kept begging for was one more chance to kill you and that brother of yours. Tonight, before I close my eyes, I know what I'll be praying for, but you"—he paused at the doorway—"you might wanna sleep with both eyes open!"

MARCO

Busting two nuts, one in Jordan's mouth making her swallow, Marco was still full on energy sparked by his need for revenge. Flicking to channel after channel he felt some twisted sense of pride in the fact that he had the entire city on lockdown. If a person living in Dallas hadn't heard about him and the multiple murders he'd committed prior to hitting Sergeant Kendricks in the head, escaping, and carjacking the city councilman, then they definitely had heard his name now.

Practically dragging Jordan into the bathroom with him to take a piss, Marco made her sit on the side of the tub and tell him everything that was going on with her and Storm. Both buck-naked, he finished off the bottle of liquor Jordan had, listening to her tell him how her sister who worked at the hospital originally called her and she planned a chance meeting with Storm. Although she wanted to be with Storm bad as hell and would do just about anything to prove her loyalty, she knew Marco was far from being a joke. Her own life being her first priority, Jordan had to survive, and if that meant temporarily throwing Storm and whoever else to the wolves, so to speak, then it was gonna happen.

"So you gotta meet up with his faggot ass, huh?" Marco sat back with a scheme brewing.

"Umm, yeah, he needs these papers."

"I wish I could go with you and just sneak that bitch with some of this act right." Marco pointed the stolen gun at Jordan trying to get his point across. "But I know the streets is too hot on my ass right about now."

Flinching seeing the gun aimed in her direction, she prayed to God. Terrified she wasn't gonna make it out of the hotel room she and Big Doc B had been committing adultery in week after week, Jordan hoped it was a Higher Power that was interested in forgiving her sins and just giving her one more chance to get her life right. "Please, Marco. Put that gun down. Why is you tripping on me?"

"I ain't tripping, bitch. I'm just speculating getting at that loser," Marco hissed after seeing the authorities had located the stolen car he'd abandoned a few blocks over.

Turning the television off in hopes of Marco calming down, Jordan tried reasoning with him. "Listen, why don't I take him the papers and see what he saying about you?" she bargained bringing up their past arrangement. "Remember all that bullshit him and O.T. used to be spitting and I put you up on? Well, you can only imagine what he saying now!"

"Yeah, you right." He finally lowered the gun.

"Well, since he call himself needing me all of a sudden because Kenya's stuck-up ass is MIA, I might as well set the fool up for you. What you think?" Jordan, a hustler by nature, knew how to play the game and say all the right things niggas wanted to hear. "Now he wouldn't ever expect to see that shit coming!"

"Maybe since that ho of his is knocked, about to drop that load, Storm might fuck around and be all in for some new pussy," Marco contemplated, sucking his teeth.

"I'm trying to tell you, he wants me." Jordan shook bargaining for her life. "It can work!"

Not knowing for sure if he could trust Jordan, Marco carefully weighed his options. On one hand, he wanted nothing more than to peel Storm's cap back, but on the other hand, it'd definitely be in his best interest to get as far away from town as he could and never look back. "You right, but how can I know your good dick-sucking ass ain't gonna turn me in as soon as I let you outside of this damn room?"

"Have I ever not had your back?" Jordan smirked and plotted. "I told you everything they asses was saying, didn't I?"

Going to the window, Marco eased over the burgundy curtain of the fifth-floor hotel room seeing several police cars circling the parking lot and swarming the streets near the building. Taking a deep breath then exhaling, Marco knew at this point he was stuck and had to make the best of a fucked-up situation he brought on himself.

Now, he just had to make sure Jordan would remain loyal to him if he let her go to play double agent. Yoking her up and shoving his gun down her throat, Marco gave her several hardcore reasons as to why she'd better keep his whereabouts on the low.

Chapter Ten

KENYA/BROTHER RASUL

Creeping down the stairs of Brother Rasul's small bungalow home, Kenya heard him speaking to someone and paused.

"Look, I already told you, it's no way in hell you gonna talk to me the way you did, let alone tell me what to do."

"You act like that's your woman, not me!" Fatima's voice cried out through his cell, which was on speaker.

Brother Rasul continued to fumble with the bassinet he'd just purchased not really caring about what she was saying. "Where is this conversation going? You gave me my keys back, so that's what it is."

"Rasul, you choosing her over me? Are you kidding me?"

After a few seconds of dead silence, Fatima regretfully got her answer.

"Yeah, I guess so." He lustfully thought about Kenya upstairs in his shower. "So go do you. I'm straight."

"You act like you wanna fuck that bitch!"

"Maybe I do, so like I said, do you!"

As the phone went dead, Kenya waited at the bottom of the stairs a good minute or so, trying to play off her blatant eavesdropping. *Damn, that was deep, but later for Fatima's good hating ass!* "Hey, Ra." Dressed in an oversized robe obviously belonging to her host, Kenya finally emerged out of the shadows, ready to face her nightmarish reality.

"Oh, hey, Kenya, you see what I got little man?" He smiled, momentarily acting as if the baby boy weren't kidnapped and his mother weren't truly dead in a walk-in freezer across the country.

Holding her robe tightly closed, Kenya sat down on the couch. Brother Rasul then ran down everything Storm had told him. He also informed her that, at this point, Storm had yet to discover London's body and she still had a chance to come clean and confess it was an accident.

"Naw, I can't go back there, and after all the grimy messages he left on me and my sister's phone, I really ain't trying to talk to him."

Wanting to gauge the situation, Brother Rasul gave her some more of his and Storm's conversation for her to think about. "Look, he sounded really worried about his brother, plus he wanted me to tell you that some dude named Marco was out of jail and they was back at war."

"Out of jail?" Kenya wondered, not even knowing he had been caught in the first place.

Brother Rasul finished assembling the bassinet. "Yeah, he told me if I did talk to you or your sister, tell both of y'all to stay outta dodge."

Kenya knew she was safe as long as Brother Rasul had her back. "Yeah, okay, but as far as me talking to him, I just don't know."

Hearing the small cries of the baby, Kenya went back upstairs to see about him as well as digest what Brother Rasul had just told her about all the hell Storm was going through. Laying the innocent infant on the bed with just a diaper on, Kenya got London's cell phone out of her purse. Focusing, she took a picture of Li'l Stone. She wrote underneath the snapshot, Our son, born today. Neither me nor my sister wants to be bothered. Kenya sent the picture and callous message to Storm. *At least his ass can see the baby he loves so much! I ain't never gonna see my sister again!*

JORDAN/STORM

I'm glad Marco decided to trust me and let me go. Jordan nervously drove up to the hospital to meet Storm. Looking around, she cautiously got out of the car wondering if what Marco claimed was indeed true. *Do he really have some nigga out here watching me and my damn sister ready to fuck us both up if I snitch him out?* Not realizing Marco had no one or no true power, she handed the valet attendant the keys as she clutched the huge envelope close to her breast.

"Hey, Storm; I'm downstairs in the lobby."

"Oh, okay then, J, come on up to the third floor. I'm on the other end handling some business."

After waiting for the elevator, Jordan gave every person getting on the evil eye, thinking they were watching her for Marco. No sooner than the third floor door slid open, Jordan saw Storm walking down the hall on his cell phone. "Hey, babe," she greeted him wanting nothing more than to blurt out that Marco Meriwether's crazy self was back at her and Big Doc B's love nest plotting to kill him.

Putting his index finger up while he was talking, Storm cracked a slightly crooked smile acknowledging Jordan's presence. "Yeah, I'ma need 'round-the-clock top-notch security on my baby brother's room." His nostrils flared as he thought about Tangy, not to mention Marco. "Gimme at least four of ya best dudes on the case. I don't give a fuck about the damn cost!" Finalizing O.T.'s safety, Storm hung up placing his cell back on his hip. "Hey, girl, what's up with you?"

Jordan fought not to tell him the truth as she saw her sister, who chose to ignore her, at the nurse's station going through some files. "Nothing, Storm, I'm chilling. Here are those papers you needed."

Sitting down in the family lobby a few yards away from O.T.'s room, Storm took the documents out the envelope. "Damn, now this here is what's really up! Thank you so much, Jordan. You don't know how much I fucking appreciate this shit." Reaching over he put his hand on her knee. "Good fucking looking out!"

Jordan was geeked, almost forgetting about Marco's threats. "It ain't nothing." She hugged him. "Hey, how is O.T. doing? Can I see him or is Kenya in there with her evil ass?"

"Kenya?" Storm repeated with complete disdain. "Naw, she ain't here. She's—"

"Hey, I heard she was pregnant," Jordan, wanting to be his fuck buddy if nothing else, interjected hoping it wasn't true.

"Kenya, pregnant? Who in the hell told you that?" Storm knew everyone in his close-knit foursome of his brother and the girls was keeping London's pregnancy a secret. So whoever heard Kenya was knocked up must've seen her twin somewhere and mistaken her for his woman. "Where you get that bullshit from?" His voice started to get louder as he stood to his feet waiting for the million dollar answer.

"Well, umm, umm . . .." Jordan knew she'd gone too far and had messed up, first by even asking about Kenya's whereabouts then, secondly, by repeating the dumb shit Marco told her. "I just thought—"

"Code red stat! Code red stat!" suddenly rang out from the nurses' station intercom. "Code red stat!"

As Nurse Jamison, Jordan's sister, along with several others on staff rushed into O.T.'s room, Storm dropped the papers he was holding on to the floor then wasted no time fighting through the crowd of caregivers getting to his brother's bedside.

"What the fuck is wrong? Help him! Help him!" Storm grabbed one doctor up by his collar. "Why are the lights flashing, huh? Why?"

"Calm down, and please let us do what we need to do!" One nurse tried shoving Storm away. "Please!"

Jordan stood over toward the side of the doorway, watching O.T.'s body jump up and down wildly as he went into cardiac arrest. Seeing the doctor roughly snatch the breathing tube out of his throat as her sister tore back the blanket, she wanted to run out of the room. Instead, in tears, Jordan held the papers Storm had dropped. Silently praying as the doctor rubbed two paddles together, she took a deep breath.

"His blood pressure is dropping!" another nurse shouted keeping her eyes glued on one of the many monitors and machines attached to O.T.'s fatigued body.

"Come on, y'all! Fuck! Help him!" Storm's eyes watered as his own heart raced and his muscles tensed up. "O.T., come on, nigga, you better than that! Pull through this, nigga! Pull through!"

Five minutes into using and doing every procedure humanly possible, the doctor in charge stepped back from the bed. Mentally beat, physically exhausted, he took off his gloves and looked downward at his wristwatch. "Sorry, everyone. Stop resuscitation efforts. I'm calling time of death at one twenty-five p.m."

"What? What? Naw! You bullshitting!" Clutching his fingers up to his forehead, Storm didn't want to hear what was just said. "All these fucking machines in here! Naw! Come on! Y'all can do something! Keep trying! It ain't over! It can't be!" In denial, he clenched his fist stomping in circles. "Come on, y'all, that's my damn brother. He all I got! Naw! Hell naw! Fuck!"

In an attempt to console Storm, the doctor sorrowfully informed him they did everything they possibly could.

"We tried. We really tried, but your brother suffered so much damage internally," he explained. "And I know this isn't the best time to bring this up, but have you ever thought about donating organs? Your brother might be able to save someone else's—"

"Motherfucker, is you fucking crazy?" Storm jumped back knocking over the pole the now useless IV bags swung from. As the needles ripped from O.T.'s arms, he went into a full-blown rage. "Y'all sons of bitches just let my baby brother die and you talking about me helping the next nigga? Fuck you and them!" Storm, with a face full of tears, took a deep breath as he reached over holding O.T.'s hand. "All of y'all get the fuck outta here and leave me and my brother alone before one of y'all lose y'all's life too!"

Knowing he was grieving, the doctors and nurses quickly left removing some of the vital machines, with the exception of Nurse Jamison. "Listen, dear, you take all the time you need." She touched his shoulder handing him some tissue. "I'll come back in a little while and check on you." As she went out of the hospital room, she paused at the doorway whispering in Jordan's ear. "See what street life gets you? Dead or in jail!"

Ignoring her sister's coldhearted but painfully true condescending words, Jordan was stunned. She was definitely feeling some sort of way. How could she not? She was human no matter how hard she would act from time to time. Jordan was a female and any woman no matter how rough and tough would be moved at this moment. Yeah, it was no big secret, she and O.T. weren't the best of friends on the outside world so to speak, but this was different. Tears had to be shed. O.T. was a straight-up nutcase and always had her back down at the strip club if anything jumped off. Out of all the bouncers at Alley Cats, O.T. was the first to stand up and the last to sit down. There was no drama that jumped off at the club or in the streets that he would back down from. If a dude wanted it with the younger Christian brother, they could get the full package strong arm pushed to them. He was a known full-blown menace, but now he was gone. What started off as a strong team of infamous criminals banding together—Storm, O.T., Deacon, and Boz—had now had the misfortunate of only one man left standing. Although that tragic information would be like music to Marco's ears, Jordan looked over at Storm who was obviously devastated.

"I feel like going down to the morgue and clowning. I'm in my zone and killing that bitch Tangy all the fuck over again for what she did to my baby brother would make me happy as hell." Storm's emotions of grief were, of course, at an all-time high. "Look at you, dude." He rubbed O.T.'s forehead fighting back more tears. "I always thought it was gonna be me and you against the world for a lifetime. Ever since back in the day when we was stealing honey buns and quarter juices out of the corner store, we been getting it. We was on some ol' Batman and Robin shit, that Green Hornet and Kato type of thang. Now, this here bullshit done jumped off. I can't believe it. I can't believe none of what done happened over the past few months. Shit is so fucked up. This is so fucked up. I swear I'm messed up right now, brother. I'm sick with it, my nigga, sick." In the midst of Storm reminiscing with his now deceased brother, his cell phone vibrated indicating a text message. Instinctively, without looking at the sender, he reached down pushing IGNORE.

From the other side of the room, Jordan's feminine compassion kicked in. Although she was a certified rotten-minded female, she was still human. Slowly, she crept to Storm's side sensing he was on the verge of reaching his breaking point. Shaking her head, she placed her hand on his shoulder. "Is it anybody you want me to call for you, Storm, like some family members or something? Who can I call?" Forgetting about Marco and his threats, the usually out-for-self dancer wanted nothing more than to be there and console her suffering, longtime acquaintance.

"Huh? Call?" Storm, who up until he'd met Kenya only really rocked with his brother and Deacon, realized he was now out here in these streets alone. Deacon was gone, O.T. was gone, and Kenya's selfish and insecure ass was also MIA. The only thing he felt he had left in the entire world was his unborn baby. "Naw, girl, it ain't nobody to call. I'm good."

"You sure, Storm?" Jordan asked already knowing the answer. "Because you know I'm here for you today, tomorrow, and always."

Seconds later, Nurse Jamison reentered the dismal, emotion-filled room. With some final papers for Storm, O.T.'s listed next of kin, to sign off on and a bag containing the deceased's personal items, she said nothing. With trembling hands trying to hold the ink pen, a devastated Storm fell to his knees throwing up his breakfast on the otherwise clean hospital room floor.

Chapter Eleven

JORDAN

"Dang, boy. Oh, my fucking God, stop sweating me like this. You bugging. I already done told you I'm on top of things. Like I told you all the other times you called last night like you crazy or something. O.T. fucking died, nigga, and Storm needed me to drive him home and handle some other thangs," she tried whispering as a dog barked continuously from the other room.

"Why his wifey can't handle that shit? And damn, bitch, stop telling me about that sucker's misfortune. Fuck O.T. I hope he rot in hellfire and double fuck Storm 'cause he gonna be reunited with his brother before the dirt gets hard in the cemetery! I got something hot for his wannabe gangster ass."

Having spent the night at Storm's condo getting drunk with him and his boy Ponytail, Jordan was feeling like Superwoman. Nothing could knock her off her square or bring her down from the life high she was feeling. Even though she passed out on the couch, she still slept under the same roof as Storm, one of the top notch playas in the city. Downing a few shots of 1800, she'd ultimately found out from Ponytail that Kenya was ghost and he hadn't seen her since he'd first gotten there. That was perfect. Jordan knew Storm was alone and vulnerable. She realized that now more than ever he needed a strong woman by his side and with Kenya gone off to wherever, this was her time to shine.

Marco, on the other hand, had been trapped in the hotel room since the day before and was growing restless. He was definitely on edge and was ready to snap. Having eaten the few candy bars, a bag of chips, and even the garden salad that came with the room service meal Jordan ordered for him before she left to meet up with Storm, he was irate. He had already taken a risk by creeping across the hall and stealing someone else's room service order left by their door. But he didn't care. He wanted exactly what he wanted when he wanted it. And putting the final nail in Storm's coffin was no exception. Truth be told, that was the force that motivated him to avoid getting apprehended. "Look, you stankin' little porch monkey, just how long you think I'm gonna sit up in this motherfucker waiting for you to snitch me out to the damn police? Do you want me to just do what I said I was gonna do and pay that nurse sister of yours a little visit? Because I can make that shit pop off real quick fast and in a hurry. Is that what you want, you cock-thirsty cunt?"

"Marco, you know what?" Jordan thought about her holier-than-thou sister and the cruel judgments she'd always passed on the lifestyles others lead. "I already done told you what was up and you could trust me. But if you feeling like coming out that motherfucker and all them cops still searching for that ass and killing my sister, then go right ahead, my nigga. You can slow kill that bitch right now. You best believe I got insurance on her ass. Matter of fact, go the fuck ahead. I need some extra money in my damn life. Do you, nigga! That's a come up waiting for me."

I got a chance to be living large with Storm, so fuck Marco! I should call the police on his black ass! After hanging up on him and transferring all calls from the hotel room number Marco called from straight to her voicemail, she continued to cook Storm and Ponytail a huge breakfast as the unfriendly dog from the rear of the kitchen area kept barking.

STORM
Selling dope, making money, and meeting the deadline he was facing were the last things on Storm's tormented mind. He couldn't care less. When his phone vibrated and the number 5 showed up, he shook his head. He'd still failed to look at the huge amount of previous texts that'd come in after word of O.T.'s tragic death spread throughout the drug-infested streets. Those texts, unfortunately, included the one Kenya sent with his newborn son's picture attached.

Nursing a hangover from the bottles of liquor he, Ponytail, and Jordan went in on and the Kush they blew, he could hardly make it to the bathroom to take a piss.

Damn O.T. He stumbled toward the stairs as he smelled the strong aroma of turkey bacon and eggs fill the air. *I need to get in touch with those dumb bitches for real.* His mind jumped to Kenya and London. Sixteen seconds later using the banister to hold himself up, both females' cells were going straight to voicemail. Angry at the world, already missing his brother who was his best friend, Storm smashed his phone against the front door breaking it almost in two. If the person who'd killed O.T. was still alive walking the streets at least Storm could have the satisfaction of murdering them and causing their family the same amount of grief he was feeling, but Malloy was right. His men had robbed him of that joy taking Tangy out. Now all he had was his pain. She didn't have any family, except for Paris, and what was the point of killing her? She was already half dead and crazy living in the nuthouse.

"Fuck the world!" Using his fist, Storm swung, punching a dent in the drywall on the side of the room. Twenty seconds later, the scent of the food cooking had him throwing up, unknowingly in the very spot his baby was born. Exhausted, not wanting to face reality, he blacked out across the couch.

JORDAN

What the fuck? Hearing a crashing sound then Storm yell something out, Jordan was puzzled. Peeping her head out the kitchen door, she saw him facedown on the couch. Not knowing if he was going through another one of his emotional breakdowns he'd gone through all night, slowly she approached him. "Hey, Storm, baby. You good?" The closer she got, the more evident it became that Storm was knocked out cold.

"Hey, girl, what's good?" Ponytail came up from the basement wiping lotion on his face. "Is that you up here making all that damn noise?"

"Naw." Jordan laughed knowing he was somewhat of an ally. "That was your manz over here." She signaled toward the couch. "That shit from last night still got him gone."

Ponytail headed to the kitchen taking in the smells of the cooked food Jordan scraped together from the few items in the refrigerator and cabinets. "Real rap, that's good. He going through some major drama right about now, ya feel me?"

"Yeah, you right. He definitely needs the rest." Jordan followed him grabbing a plate. "Well, while he sleeping, it ain't no need for you to miss out on this breakfast."

Ponytail went in the far side of the kitchen. "Hey, Reckless, hey, boy! Here come daddy!" He cracked the door open letting the pit bull see his familiar face.

Watching him jump up and down, Jordan backed away from the animal whose head and body were as big as a small pony. "Get him, get him!"

"Girl, stop tripping, you good."

"Naw, fuck that." Jordan eased near the doorway not ever wanting to go in that direction. "I don't play with no damn dogs."

When Ponytail was finished feeding his four-legged companion and letting him run around the fenced-in backyard, he finally fixed himself a plate. Not wasting any more time when he was done, he snatched his keys off the coffee table. "You listen up. I know you probably mad busy with shit to do, but ol' boy need somebody to stay with him. One of us can make sure we pick his car up from the hospital."

"It ain't no problem, but what about his girl Kenya?"

Ponytail was on a mission. Having to pick up the ticket money from several trap houses, Storm's childhood friend was short, brief, and to the point. "Look, like I told you last night, I ain't seen her since I been here, so just look out 'til I get back okay?"

Jordan finished cleaning up the kitchen as Storm snored away on the couch, still dead to the world. Having spent the night on the couch, she had yet to see the rest of the condo Kenya, whom she hated, had the privilege to call home. Making her way up the stairs, she admired the color scheme along with the extravagant pictures that were hung tastefully on the walls. Peeping her head inside the first bedroom, her jaw dropped. *This must be the master bedroom. They living like fucking kings.* Overlooking the clothes tossed around, broken picture frame glass, and overall messiness, Jordan was still very much jealous. In between dope and Alley Cats, Storm was getting it.

Not caring if Storm awoke and came upstairs to find her snooping, Jordan strolled into one of the walk-in closets, discovering what appeared to be all of Kenya's expensive wardrobe thrown about. *Wherever her stupid ass at, I sure wouldn't have left this.* She held a dress up to her body. *Or this.* She picked up another.

Minutes after being nosey in there, she went down the hallway discovering the room London had been sleeping in. *What the fuck?* Picking up baby clothes off the floor and prenatal care books off the dresser, Jordan was confused and amazed. *Okay, so that bitch Kenya is pregnant. So what's the big secret? And why Storm get so defensive about the bullshit?* Looking over at the bed and all the personal items that sat on the nightstand, she then started to laugh. *Oh, hell naw, don't tell me him and that stuck-up bitch been sleeping in separate rooms!*

Twenty or so minutes into playing detective, Jordan finally went back downstairs before Storm woke up or Ponytail came back. By the looks of what she's just seen, Kenya showing up anytime soon was the last thing on her mind.

MARCO

"That good dick-sucking trick got some damn nerve hanging up on me." Marco slammed the receiver of the hotel room's desk phone down and grabbed his pistol. "I got a right mind to leave up out this motherfucker and kill her punk-ass sister for real! She must think I'm one of them tricks she mind fucks down at that club. I ain't the one. I'll put something real hot up in her for real."

Pacing, agitated, he picked up an empty bottle of liquor off the floor hoping he'd be blessed with maybe a corner he could kill off. Turning it up and not getting so much as a taste he got angrier as he clicked on the television to the morning news. *I swear, if them police wasn't still looking for my black ass, I'd be out, because that ho Jordan is bugging! She straight trying it with me. I'm a boss out in them streets; nothing more nothing less.*

Having to take a leak, Marco set his gun down on the minibar before going into the bathroom. Trying to come up with a master plan to murder Storm, then get out of town not captured and alive, Marco paused almost in mid-piss as he heard the room door handle move, then push open. *What the fuck?*

"Hey, Miss Lady!" a man's voice shouted out obviously now inside the room. "Damn what's been going on in here? I need to call housekeeping." He made reference to the over-the-top mess and disregard for the hotel room. "You do know this room is rented, don't you? Come on out that bathroom so we can talk. And why did you have that DO NOT DISTURB sign on the door? What was that about?"

As the voice got louder and the questions kept coming, Marco was frozen. *I must've left that double lock off when I cuffed that fucking food.* He was trapped in the bathroom and knew his only option would be to shoot his way out. *Shit!* he thought, quickly realizing his pistol was on the other side of the door.

"Jordan? Hey, Jordan!" Big Doc B yelled toward the semi-shut bathroom door. "Bring your ass out here! I'm about to call somebody up here to clean this mess before I end up paying an arm and a leg for permanent damages. This don't make no type of sense. You need to be ashamed of yourself." Reaching for the phone that was sitting on the nightstand, he was hotter than fish grease. "I have never seen this side of you. Do you keep your apartment like this? Because if you do, it's a wonder you haven't caught some sort of disease. This is terrible."

Before he could get an answer from Jordan or push the number nine button for the front desk, he paused. Something shiny caught his attention. Raising his brow, he noticed what looked like a gun across the room on top of the empty minibar. Placing the receiver down on the hook, he walked over to investigate. As he stood with his back to the bathroom, he was confused. First not believing the nasty condition of the room and now noticing a huge revolver in plain sight, Doc started to feel like something was very wrong.

"What in the hell?" Big Doc B's hand reached for the long-barrel pistol with the wood-grain handle. Before he knew what was happening next, he felt a strong, painful force come crashing down on the rear portion of his skull. Big Doc B lifted his hands up to shield from whatever was causing the impromptu pain. That didn't stop the mysterious attack. Matter of fact, it increased the blows rendering him disoriented. His legs grew weak. He was barely standing. As his fingertips and knuckles became drenched in what he knew had to be his own blood, Big Doc B attempted to turn around. Like clockwork, he was then met by some other object smashing into the dead center of his forehead. Immediately a huge gash opened up, and blood started to leak down. His eyes were quickly covered. He fought to stay alert and in the moment, but he couldn't. His body collapsed on the floor right next to a pile of dirty towels.

Nursing a massive headache from the metal towel rack used to knock him out cold, Doc soon regained consciousness. Focusing his eyes, he was face to face with the infamous Marco Meriwether who he'd seen breaking news alerts about all morning on every channel. Tied up with strips of the bed sheets, Doc was helpless. Struggling to break free or at least get the tight gag off his mouth was amusing to his captor as Marco sat across the room smiling.

"Come on now, you know you about hit so just fall back," Marco calmly advised while fumbling with Doc's phone. "You's just wasting your time. I used some of them dumb-ass Boy Scouts knots they taught at them old welfare summer camps. So look, old dude, chill!"

Knowing he was 100 percent correct, Doc stopped moving all together. He breathed hard, and his eyes showed fear. *Why did I come over here? Why didn't I just go straight to the office?* He searched the room wondering if Jordan was tied up in the bathroom somewhere or if she was part of Marco's mayhem.

Scrolling down Doc's contacts, he came up with several familiar numbers. "Damn, nigga. Storm, Kenya, O.T., which you can delete." He laughed. "And of course our girl Jordan. Alley Cats, Bare Faxx, The Hot Box, shit! You got all the strip clubs on speed dial." Moments later he searched through Doc's text messages to pass the time. Suddenly, Marco's eyes widened. "Oh, hell naw! Let me watch this freak shit again!" Marco couldn't believe what he was seeing. "Hold up, is this you getting some head from Storm's wifey? Your flabby ass fucking around with Jordan and that uppity ho Kenya?"

Temporarily forgetting about the immediate danger he was facing at Marco's hands, Doc squirmed around, terrified what Storm would do to him if he ever saw the video Kenya recorded.

"That bitch going in ain't she? Dang, why ain't you bang them guts?" After watching, the "Tastey Does Doc" video show a few more times, Marco's demented laughter got louder and his comments got harsher. "Oh, snap, do Storm's gangster-wannabe pimp ass know you giving his girl the dick all up in her head? I'm about to send him this bullshit right fucking now and see what a boss he think he is then!"

Chapter Twelve

KENYA

Lying in Brother Rasul's king-sized bed, Kenya started to wonder why Storm hadn't responded to the picture message she'd sent him of his newborn son. Yeah, she knew the text she'd sent underneath it was cold, harsh, and straight to the point, but that still wouldn't have stopped him from calling back talking shit, not to London, whose cell she sent it from and certainly not to her. *He probably planning some ol' crazy Rambo stunt. Shit, his ass probably searching every hotel in Dallas.*

After a few minutes, her mindset shifted. *Maybe he found London and know it's some shit behind that text. Maybe he called the police and they looking for me.* Kenya immediately erased that thought knowing him turning her in to the law would be like turning himself in. She pulled the thin blanket up over her head, and her stomach growled as she thought about the good dinner Rasul had prepared for her the evening prior. *That stupid ho Fatima don't know how good she had it. She had a dude cooking for her and looking out financially, not to mention trustworthy, not cheating. If I could turn back the hands of time for me and Storm, I would in a heartbeat.*

Just as Kenya was replaying Brother Rasul's conversation/argument he'd had with Fatima, especially the part of him saying he wanted to fuck her, she heard him walking up the stairs. "Hey, you."

"Hey, Kenya, how was your nap?"

"It was good. I'm sorry I'm putting you out your bed." Kenya sat up as he came over toward her. "I told you I can sleep in your spare room."

"Naw, don't be silly, queen. You and li'l man is my guests."

"Thanks, Ra. When I woke up, I saw he was out his bassinet, so I figured you had him downstairs."

"Yeah, me and him was doing a little male bonding," he announced. "He's asleep on the couch with a pillow around him, but I need to talk to you about something important."

Oh, damn, here we go. Kenya held the covers tightly. "What is it? Did Storm call again?"

"Naw, it wasn't Storm. It was one of my people out there. They had an update for me."

"An update?" Kenya puzzled.

Brother Rasul sat down on the edge of the bed. "Listen, Kenya. Apparently Storm's brother O.T. died late yesterday afternoon."

"What! Are you serious?" she shouted constantly surrounded by death and mayhem. "Not him too?"

Brother Rasul held Kenya in his arms as she started to sob. "Listen, queen, I need you to hold it together because I need to ask you something."

Wiping her face, Kenya looked into his eyes. "What is it?"

Cupping her face in his hands, Brother Rasul started his speech. "I know you and Storm ain't on the best of terms, and I know you scared, and whenever he discovers your sister's body in that freezer he's gonna nut up even more, but that man gonna need you and your strength now more than ever. He's gonna want his son with him. Don't you think you owe him that much?"

Kenya was confused. She was hurt. And most of all she was worried. As long as she was in Detroit, with Brother Rasul, she was safe. Kenya knew for certain he wouldn't let anyone or anything hurt her. "I don't know."

"Listen, you need to make amends. You know you can't keep that man's seed away from him forever. I mean if he is anything like me, sooner or later he gonna find a way to be with him."

Laying her head on his shoulder, Kenya smelled the scent of his cologne, which happened to be one of Storm's favorites. Distraught and feeling lost, she pressed her wet face into Brother Rasul's neck. She held him closely, and Kenya's lips softly kissed his neck once, then twice. Before the both of them knew it, the friends were going at it like teenagers. Hands here and there and everywhere. Tongues were on every part of each other's body, and sweat and lust exploded on the sheets.

An hour later, the two so-called friends lay, bodies entangled, in the king-sized bed confused over what had just happened. The fact that Kenya told him she was still bleeding, the fact that she had let her sister die, and the fact that she'd just days before slept with Storm meant absolutely nothing to Brother Rasul. All of Fatima's disrespectful insults had come to be true. He did have feelings for Kenya, and he'd go against anything or any-one to make her happy, even his religion, which forbids having sexual intercourse with a woman during her time of the month.

Hearing the baby crying, he sat up. "I'll be right back. Let me get little man."

When he stood to his feet, Kenya took a deep breath staring at his tall, chiseled frame but her mind was back in Dallas and the life she'd just run away from. "Damn," she mumbled holding the sheet up to her body watching him leave the room. "I wonder what Storm is doing? I hope he's okay. I know he's fucked up in the head right about now."

Moments later, a now robed Brother Rasul returned with the baby in his arms and a bottle in his hand. Sitting down in the La-Z-Boy near the bed, he fed the infant as Kenya bit at her nails. "Look, when I finish feeding this baby, we gotta straighten this bullshit out, okay? You gotta face the music."

"Yeah, but—"

"But nothing, Kenya. This mess is serious, and I need to get a hold on it before it gets so far gone I can't do shit!" He slightly raised his voice. "Besides, you just can't leave your sister's body like that. She deserves better don't you think? If you walk away like that, you gonna regret it later, trust me."

"Okay, well—" Before Kenya could say any more, they were interrupted by the ringing of Brother Rasul's cell phone, which was sitting on the nightstand.

STORM

After sleeping half the day away, Storm woke up still feeling the depressing thoughts associated with losing his brother. Taking a shower and going back downstairs, he found Ponytail sitting on the couch eating a sandwich that Jordan had made for him before she left earlier. "Hey, man."

"Hey, Storm, what's going on? You good or what?" Ponytail set the plate on the coffee table and turned the television on mute.

"Yeah, I'm just fucked up at this whole dumb-ass bullshit that's all." He sat in his favorite chair reflecting. "One minute a nigga here talking shit, smoking weed, and chasing behind hoes and just like that, bam, a nigga dead and gone. It's crazy."

Ponytail, like the night before, was at a loss for words. "I feel you, man. O.T., me, and you had some wild times back in the day."

For the first time in days, Storm laughed. "Hell yeah. Matter of fact, I'm surprised all three of our black asses ain't dead! We used to take this city through it!"

"Yeah, back in the day." Ponytail thought about his girl at home and his kids. "But shit done changed for me. Well, at least up until now."

"And straight up, dawg, a guy like me really appreciate you helping a nigga out in his time of need. Especially since ol' girl is MIA."

Not wanting to be nosey or in the next man's business, Ponytail finally asked Storm where Kenya was at while they counted out the ticket money on the floor. Storm was hesitant at first, but he knew he owed his boy some sort of explanation as to why he was alone without his supposed fiancée by his side. As the jaded story unfolded, Ponytail sat stunned that almost stupid streetwise Kenya had a secret goody-goody twin who had lived back in Detroit without Storm's knowledge. He was even more speechless that Storm had fucked around and dicked the wrong sister down, knocking her up.

"Dude, you have no idea how crazy that bullshit was and how it jumped off. After that misunderstanding with Javier's savage ass, I was messed up on painkillers like a motherfucker and drinking myself damn near to death. A brother was depressed like some old Lifetime movie them females so strung out on. Shidddd, I slipped up one night. Then bam, Kenya sister let that shit come out one night after we was beefing. Dawg, it was madness around this place."

"You know what, Kenya? From day one right off rip, I should've known that you was gonna be trouble. My little brother warned me about dealing with you, but

I wouldn't listen. Now it's about to be a damn all-out street war because you and your sidekick Paris fucked the fuck up and killed that girl for nothing! The streets of Dallas gonna run red for this shit! I'm done with your ass for real this time! You costing me way too much!"

Kenya went into hysterics as she started throwing dishes against the wall and begging for Storm's forgiveness once again. Having no self-respect, the once Detroit diva was crawling on her knees pleading with him not to leave her. London, stunned, was now pissed as she watched her own flesh and blood lower herself by this pathetic display.

"Kenya! Get up off that damn floor! His cheating ass ain't worth humiliating yourself like this! Get up!"

"And as for you, bitch, I 'bout done had enough of your instigating ass too! Why don't you pack your bags and get to stepping with her bad-luck ass!" Storm ran up in London's face like he wanted to swing. "Get your funky ass the fuck out my house!"

"Slow down, Storm! This is my sister's house too!" London fired back standing her ground.

"Well, Kenya, you gonna tell this tramp to be ghost or what?" Storm waited with a smirk on his face. "It's me or her, and I'm not playing around this time!" It grew quiet in the room as all eyes were on Kenya, who was breathing hard wiping the tears from her eyes. After a long pause, she finally mumbled.

"What did you say?" Storm demanded to hear. "Speak up, we can't hear you!"

"I said, London, would you mind getting a hotel room somewhere until me and Storm figure all of this mess out?" Kenya, ashamed of what she'd just asked, failed to look at her twin sister. "Please, sis, it'll only be for a few days, I promise, until we work stuff out!"

"Naw, make that forever!" Storm shouted in response to Kenya's question to her sister.

"Oh, it's like that?" London was heated over what Kenya said. "I've put my life on hold for you for months, and now you're taking his side over mine! How could you?"

"Please, London!" Kenya whimpered not wanting to face or hear the truth. "Please!"

Storm started to laugh and couldn't help himself as he taunted his woman's sister. "You heard her now didn't you? So go pack your shit and leave so I can get back to my life."

"Yeah, okay! Not at all a problem!" London headed up the stairs and to her room to gather her belongings. "You two deserve each other! I don't know how I stayed here in this madhouse this long anyhow!" she yelled as she tossed her clothes and a few personal items in a bag.

When she came back down Storm and Kenya were sitting on the couch talking. He was still dogging Kenya out, but he stopped to sneer at London's seeming fall from grace. "Don't worry. I already called your silly jealous ass a cab, so you can just go wait on the damn curb!"

Kenya was silent as London passed by and went into the kitchen to get something else before struggling to drag her bags to the front door. Just as she opened the front door, the cab was pulling up and blew once. London looked back at her twin giving her one last chance to change her mind. "You sure about this, Kenya? You're picking this slimeball dope dealer over me?"

Kenya lowered her head in embarrassment over what was apparently her decision. After all she and London had been through and stuck together, the sisterly love and bond they shared was now being torn apart.

"Okay, so you know what it is, bitch. Now kick rocks." Storm held the door open. "And don't bother us again. Kenya will call you so don't call her, you lonely ho!"

London was really overjoyed to leave. She'd suffered through just about enough of Storm's disrespectful mouth not to mention Kenya's spineless demeanor. With all her bags on the porch, she spitefully turned around to face her sister and the man she'd so easily chosen over their bond. Vindictively London pulled up her T-shirt exposing a secret of her own that would shut a boisterous Storm up once and for all. Rubbing her slightly pudgy stomach in a circular motion looking down, London grinned delivering the show-stopping revelation of the evening thus far.

"It's all good this way. Don't worry about me. And trust, I ain't gonna be lonely for long, believe that!" London smirked as all eyes were on her rubbing her belly. "Tell your auntie Kenya and daddy Storm bye!"

"I don't understand! What the fuck are you talking about, London?" Kenya broke her silence running over to the door following her sister out to the cab. "What you mean daddy Storm? What is you talking about?"

Storm frowned after reliving the night that changed his life forever. "Damn it was crazy and now all this aftermath of bullshit to go with it."

"Dang, guy, and I thought I had thangs hard trying to live the nine-to-five life!" Ponytail cut their conversation short when the evening news came on with, of course, coverage of Marco Meriwether's brazen escape and assault taking the lead. "This fool probably halfway to Mexico by now."

"With him, it ain't no telling. That's why I told my girl and her sister to stay underneath the radar."

"Yeah, Storm, I feel you on all that, but don't you need somebody to help you with the funeral arrangements?"

Storm paused for a minute, but he knew until Marco was caught, dead, or at least spotted halfway across the world, it was best for the ones close to him—Kenya, London, and his unborn child—to remain out of dodge.

"Yeah, I do need somebody, but that's what I got Jordan's big-titty, wide ass around for. That bitch is a Ryder! So let her do what she do best: ride for a nigga! She expendable like a motherfucker, but my family ain't. I already done lost my blood. Besides, when it comes down to it, ain't none of them hoes paying the tab for my baby brother's final day." He snatched a few stacks off the floor. "That tab is all mine! But I do need to check on Kenya's crazy ass."

"I heard that. I'ma bust up and give you a minute." Ponytail got up after the final count was fourteen stacks, mostly fives and tens. Shaking his head thinking about the twisted situation his boy was facing, he went into the kitchen. "Yo, do you. I need to go feed Reckless anyhow. He gets real ugly when he misses meals."

Using the house phone, Storm dialed Brother Rasul's cell after Kenya and London failed to answer theirs.

"Yeah, hello." Storm headed on the front porch looking up at the late evening stars then over at the spot his brother was supposedly shot at.

"Hey, Storm," Brother Rasul replied seemingly shocked to hear Storm's voice. "What's going on your way? How's your brother doing?" He played it off not wanting him to know he had people out in Dallas giving him updates on all of his activities.

Storm lowered his head. "Yeah, well, um, shit my way is fucked up. My little brother gone. He didn't make it."

"Gone? Are you serious?" Brother Rasul held the phone being as sympathetic as possible considering he just had sex with Storm's woman. "I'm sorry to hear that. If it's anything I can do, let me know."

"Well, it is two things a nigga, sorry, I mean a guy needs."

"Speak on it." Brother Rasul sat on the edge of the bed caressing a nervous Kenya.

"Well, first things first, have you heard from my girl? I need to let her and London know about O.T. I know the news is all over town by now, but I need to kick it to both of them personally, you feel me?"

"Yeah, I feel you," Brother Rasul agreed moving his hand up to Kenya's face. "I talked to her earlier and when we hang up I'ma make sure she calls you, okay?"

"All right, cool." Storm knew Brother Rasul's word was bond, so if he said he was gonna make sure Kenya called, then she was definitely gonna call. "And the other thing is, since I'm dealing with my brother and all this madness, not to mention Marco's dumb ass, I was wondering if—"

Brother Rasul easily read in between the lines and knew where Storm's next statement was going. Wasting no time, he cut him off. "Hold up for a minute. If you gonna ask me anything about you and them boys," he said, knowing low-key that Storm understood who he was referring to, "then don't! I told you when I first hooked that situation up, it was no turning back. And I know for a fact they had to have told you that too."

"Yeah, I ain't gonna lie. It was told to me, but I damn straight ain't expect my brother to be out the picture and me having to plan a fucking funeral and cash it all the way out!"

"You didn't have a policy on your brother?"

"Hell naw! Me and him was planning on life, not goddamn death!"

Brother Rasul was torn, but the game was the game. And Storm freely chose to play it, so now no matter what jumped off, he just had to roll with the punches. "I feel your pain, but real talk, it ain't much I can do. Try putting some extra people on the streets and grind out as much cash as you can."

"I think I'ma have enough dough to make that first payment, but I need Kenya to run me back that money she stole. Normally I wouldn't trip, especially since I know she's hurt about me and London having a baby together, but I need that money bad."

"Look, Storm," Brother Rasul wisely advised, "I tell you what. Hang up and let me get with Kenya. Then maybe y'all can come to some sort of an agreement. I know for a fact she needs to speak to you as bad as you need to speak to her."

"All right, bet."

Brother Rasul hung up the phone and looked at Kenya who was trying her best to get dressed. Part of him wanted to say fuck Storm, he wanted her for himself, but the Muslim in him said to at least give the man a fighting chance. "Hold up, Kenya. You just heard me tell him you were going to call. Now slow your roll and call the brother. He straight going through it. So here."

Slowly taking the cell out his hands, she pushed *67 before calling Storm's cell. "It went to his voicemail." Relieved, she wasn't off the hook as Brother Rasul instructed her to try again. "No, sorry, voicemail again."

"Well, try this number." He scrolled down his caller ID. "This is the number he just called me from."

Dialing the number she recognized as the house line, Kenya got an answer. "Hello."

"Kenya, baby, is this you?" Storm was a broken man in spirit when he heard her cracking voice. "Hello."

"Yeah, it's me," she spoke softly while twisting her hair through her fingertips. "What's going on?"

"First things first, yo. I'm sorry all them lies I been telling. I ain't mean that bullshit, it's just that, well, you know."

"Naw, Storm, I don't know. Tell me." Kenya tried hard swallowing the lump in her throat.

"O.T. is dead, baby! He's dead! That crazy bitch Tangy killed him!"

"I know." She closed her eyes listening to him fall apart. "I heard."

"I can't fucking believe how shit done turned out!" Storm knew he had to choose his words carefully, especially since Kenya might bug out and hang up. "A nigga was just trying to do what I thought was best. I wasn't trying to hurt nobody and now you gone, my brother gone, and—"

"Don't say it." Kenya stopped him before he mentioned her sister or the baby. "Didn't you get the picture message?"

Storm was confused. "Picture? What picture?"

"The one from London's phone." Kenya's voice started to tremble even more. "The one with your son."

"My son?" Storm stood to his feet. "What you talking about, Kenya? Where is London?"

At that point in the conversation, Kenya realized, amazingly, he still hadn't gone into the walk-in freezer and discovered her twin. Maybe Brother Rasul was correct and she could make things right with Storm. Maybe he could forgive her callousness and they could be a family. "Umm . . ." She stumbled over answering the question. "She, umm . . ."

"Kenya," Storm yelled wanting to know exactly what she meant saying "his son." "Kenya, did you say son? Where is London? Put her on the line! I ain't bullshitting around no more! I know she didn't have my baby and y'all both trying to say fuck me!"

Anger and frustration reentered Kenya's mindset as her blood started to boil. "Oh, damn, there go the selfish son of a crackhead Storm I know! I knew that 'I'm sorry' bullshit wasn't gonna last."

"Look, bitch!"

"Bitch? Bitch? Oh, yeah, I got your bitch, bitch!"

"Listen, Kenya, stop playing games and put London on the line. If I find out she had my son and y'all keeping him from me then—"

"Then what?" Now up on her feet walking around the once quiet room, her loud tone startled the baby, who started to cry.

"Is that my son I hear in the background? Is it? I hear a baby!"

Kenya, still feeling some sort a way about how she'd been mistreated by him over the past nine months, was over it. Having had about enough of Storm, she let him have it full blast. "Yeah, fool, that's your fucking son! Hell motherfucking yeah! And guess what, even if Marco wasn't hunting your black ass down and I was staying out of dodge, you still wouldn't be able to see this baby, trust!"

Storm was overjoyed she'd informed him that London had given birth, but he was way past the point of kissing her ass. "Look, I need to speak to London. What hospital she at? And then I need for your dumb ass to run me my money! You think you just gonna gangster my shit? I need that shit!"

"Fall back! People in hell need ice water, so now what?" Pushing the END button, Kenya was done talking to Storm. Any thoughts she had of a happily ever after ending were over. With twisted lips, she waited for Brother Rasul to say anything positive, which she didn't want to hear, and the baby continued to cry.

Storm, regretting the fact he smashed his cell breaking it in two pieces, hated he couldn't see any pictures of his newborn son. First order of business the next morning would be buying a replacement phone.

Chapter Thirteen

JORDAN

Enjoying a good night's sleep in her own apartment, Jordan awoke with a serious official "I don't give a damn about jack shit" attitude. Having dreamt about what she'd do with the life insurance money she'd inherit if Marco made good on his threat of murdering her sister, Jordan finished getting dressed. Throwing on a tight-fitting jogging suit and a pair of flip-flops, she got ready for the long but much anticipated prearranged day she was gonna spend with Storm running errands.

Already planning on making herself at home at his condo, Jordan packed a small duffle bag with a few essentials, not to mention a couple of "ho items" (tricks of her trade) that could possibly take Storm's mind off the grief he was suffering. Even though she felt like Ponytail had been giving her the eye, low-key, the night before, Storm was definitely the hog with the big nuts. He was the main catch, the one who could change her lifestyle and status citywide. And now that Kenya had fallen off, for whatever reason, Jordan was set on taking advantage of the situation.

I hope that ho Kenya and that baby of hers stay ghost. By the time she do get her shit together and try coming back, Storm gonna be my man.

Removing her cell from the charger, Jordan wasn't shocked seeing the small symbol in the corner of the screen indicating that she had multiple voice messages. After she'd hung up on Marco the day before, telling him to basically kick rocks, eat shit, and die, the feisty female expected nothing less. Putting her phone on speaker as she fixed her hair in the mirror, she giggled as she listened to the numerous threats, one by one.

One: "Bitch, pick up this motherfucking phone! I ain't playing with your stanking ass! You playing games like a nigga ain't got no juice to reach out and touch your ugly ass!"

Two: "You think this shit is a damn joke, ho! You think you doing something with your good nut-swallowing ass! Call me the fuck back!"

Three: "Your sister dead, bitch, and so the fuck is you! I'ma catch that stuck-up bitch coming out that hospital and smoke her ass, watch! Pick up this damn phone, trick!"

Four: "You got me all the way fucked up! You think a nigga can't get at you, huh? Is that what you think, ho? I got something for you. I swear on my life, bitch, I'ma see you!"

Five: "Oh, you hanging with Storm. You think he can save you? Bitch, y'all both dead!"

Repeatedly, one after the other, they kept coming; number six , number seven , number eight. The pissed-off sound of Marco's voice echoed throughout the bathroom walls a good ten minutes or so before Jordan's voicemail inbox was completely empty. "You have no more new messages." All the name calling, insults, threats, and promises about bringing harm to both her and her older sister meant absolutely nothing to Jordan. As far as she was concerned, Marco was lucky she hadn't just called the damn police and turned his black ass in the minute she safely got in the hotel's lobby and out of his reach.

But instead, for old times' sake, even though he dogged her, the general code of the street life she insisted on living in was she didn't snitch his treacherous ass out. Jordan, now caught up with being Storm's next wifey, decided to let the police do what they got paid to do: hunt Marco down on their own.

Checking her watch, Jordan gathered a few more items and left her apartment. Cautious, but relieved Marco didn't know where she laid her head at, since she only tricked with dudes at rooms, him being there was not even a possibility. On her own mission, she didn't feel the need to look over her shoulder. *Forget that asshole! If he know what I know, he need to get outta dodge, before I change my mind!*

With just enough time to get a pedicure before meeting up with Storm, Jordan jumped in her car, turned up the radio, and sped to the nail salon forgetting about every vile message Marco left.

MARCO

"Can you believe this foul-smelling pussy skank call herself going hard and not picking up?" Marco looked down in the bathtub at Big Doc B, who was still tied up. Having forced him to sleep there all night, Marco had no problem whatsoever taking out his dick and taking an early morning piss right in front of his victim. "She don't know who she dealing with!"

Doc was exhausted from trying his best to break free all night long. Dealing with a massive headache from the towel rack that had knocked him out, along with a severe cramp in his left leg, all he could do was what he'd been doing throughout the duration of the night: pray he made it out of this ordeal alive and back to his family.

"That tramp think she's so fucking smart, but I got a idea that's gonna make her ass come right to me." Marco schemed shaking his dick twice before putting it back inside his pants. "Oh, yeah, and I almost forgot. Your damn wife called your cell at least ten or fifteen times." He laughed out loud as Doc's eyes grew wider. "I texted her that your mouth was full of some slut's pussy and you couldn't talk! Plus I sent her your special edition video."

Hearing that gave Doc a new sudden burst of energy to get home to his family, but unfortunately, it wasn't enough for him to get loose.

"Yo, my nigga, stop all that wiggling around and shit while I get ready. I need to hurry up and bump heads with Jordan real, real soon. I need to show that goofy tramp my pimp hand is still strong!"

Turning on the morning news, Marco surprisingly learned there had been several alleged sightings of him on the far side of town at least ten miles away from the hotel. *Damn, they dumb as a fuck!*

Knowing the already economically stressed law enforcement department would be focusing in on that particular area of the city, he knew this was his perfect opportunity to make his escape from the room. Using Doc's cell, he sent another text. Tucking the police-issued pistol down in his pants, Marco grabbed Doc's lightweight jacket off the floor putting it on. With Doc's wallet, jewelry, cell phone, and car keys, Marco raised the metal towel bar once more crashing it against Doc's skull and rendering him unconscious. Creeping out into the hallway, he put the DO NOT DISTURB sign on the doorknob to buy him some time before someone actually came into the room and discovered he'd been hiding out there.

Placing Big Doc B's designer sunglasses on his face in hopes of somewhat disguising himself, Marco exited the hotel and went toward the parking lot. *Hell yeah, I'm out that motherfucker!* With the BMW specialty cut keys in hand, easily he spotted the coupe. Using the keychain alarm, Marco clicked it unlocking the doors. *Now let's see how much bullshit Jordan gonna be talking.* He used Doc's cell phone once again before pulling out the hotel parking lot.

JORDAN
Opting to get a French manicure on her toes, Jordan sat back relaxing while daydreaming about being a kept woman just like Kenya had been over the past year. In the middle of her conniving thoughts, the feeling of her cell vibrating snatched her back to the moment. *What the fuck?* she immediately wondered reading the new text message. *This ain't this fool's day to be on my trail.* Typing back her response quickly, there was no way she was gonna turn down money, especially free money.
Where r u at?
In d-town area.
Happily waiting for her toes to dry a little before getting up, Jordan smiled when Big Doc B texted her back telling exactly where she could meet up with him and pick up the extra cash he'd won from a high-stakes card game he'd played the evening prior. She texted back, Roger that! Doc was always doing a little this and that for her from time to time, so this donation to her ghetto-balling lifestyle was, of course, welcome and not a surprise.
I'm glad he didn't say the hotel room, because that spot is definitely a thang of the past until Marco is locked back up and out the way. She slipped on her flip-flops, tipped the Korean woman, and headed toward the door. *Matter of fact, I'ma tell Doc, for the time being, he can just let that room go. Besides, Storm's fine ass about to be paying all my bills.*
Pulling her car into the semi-deserted parking lot in the back of an office building, Jordan saw the rear of Doc's Beemer. Glancing at the dashboard clock, she

knew she only had ten maybe fifteen minutes top to kick it with Doc's tricking ass before she had to be on her way to meet up with Storm at his condo. Parking directly next to his car, Jordan looked in her mirror, making sure her makeup was cute, before jumping out. Prancing over to the vehicle with dark tinted windows, without looking inside first she eased inside shutting the door in one seemingly fast motion. Seconds later, caught completely off guard, she felt Marco's rough hands wrapped around her throat, squeezing.

"Yeah, you stupid ho! What was that shit you was blowing out your grill last night?" His grip tightened as she struggled. "You's a boss bitch, right? Right? So boss the fuck up now!"

Gasping for air, Jordan's hands tugged at her attacker's trying to get away. The more she pulled, the harder Marco seemed to bear down. Fighting for her life, she used the only thing she had for a weapon: her fingernails. Wildly reaching up, Jordan clawed deep into Marco's skin gouging a huge chunk of skin from each side of his cheeks momentarily causing him to let up.

"Nooo, nooo, stop!" She leaned on the passenger door hoping it would magically open and she could escape.

Feeling the stinging from the scratches, Marco retaliated by two strong palm smacks across her face. "Shut the fuck up!" he demanded finally reaching between his legs revealing his gun. "If I gotsta say that shit again, I'ma put something hot up in your brains besides this good dick you use to having there, you feel me?"

Scared out her mind, Jordan did as she was told. With a face full of tears and nursing a now sore neck, she breathed in and out rapidly. "Why you doing this?" she managed to ask.

"Yo, for real, are you kidding me?" Marco wanted to just smoke her and be done with it, but he knew she had information he needed to follow through on his plans to kill Storm before he left town. "Ain't you the one who told me to go fuck myself yesterday? I should leave you right in the back seat of this bitch with two to the head."

Jordan started to shake. "Please, Marco, please. I'm sorry. I didn't mean it. I promise I didn't."

After listening to the once mouthy female beg, plead, and bargain for her life, Marco told her what he wanted from her and what she was gonna do from this point on if she wanted to live. Terrified, now realizing he could reach out and touch her at any time, Jordan swore she would tell him any and all moves Storm made the next few days. She started by letting him know exactly what funeral home Storm talked about contacting the night of O.T.'s death.

"I'm everywhere, bitch, know that! And if you even think about turning me the fuck in, I ain't housing at that hotel no more. I left that old, slick getting-pussy nigga there taking a bath." Marco sarcastically smirked referring to Doc. "But don't worry, he alive. After watching this, I had to let the OG live!" Marco let Jordan watch the video once before laying down his law and letting her go. "Remember what I said, bitch! I'm every-fucking-where!"

Safely back inside her car, Jordan took at least a good twenty minutes getting herself back together before even trying to call Storm and let him know she was finally on her way. *Kenya's tramp ass been fucking around with Doc all this time.* Jordan rubbed her neck with one hand while steering with the other. *I wonder does Storm know and damn, is that baby Kenya having even his? Maybe that's why she left.*

Engulfed in the various scenarios that could've brought Kenya and Doc together in the first place, Jordan finally showed some compassion for someone other than herself: Doc. *Marco got Doc's keys and pushing his ride. I hope he's alive like Marco said.* With a shaky voice looking in her rearview mirror to see if she was being followed, Jordan dialed the hotel's front desk. Anonymously, she informed the manager on duty there had been some sort of an accident in room 521 and someone on staff needed to enter to premises to look into it.

Realizing housekeeping hadn't been allowed to enter and clean room 521 for over three days straight and counting, the manager believed Jordan's claim and personally went himself to investigate.

BIG DOC B

Trying his best to hold on to life, Doc heard the paramedics talking to him as he was stretched out on the floor of the hotel room, but he couldn't open his eyes or mouth to respond. With each second passing their voices got further and further away. Soon he heard nothing. All Big Doc B's cheating indiscretions, marital contempt, and all-night trips to strip clubs were over. The fact that he had this love nest rented for months at a time wouldn't be able to be questioned. Those actions along with the consequences he would've inevitably been faced to deal with from his longtime devoted and extremely jealous wife, who was already diagnosed as being clinically depressed and Storm when the video was finally discovered were going to be taken to the grave with him. Thank God for that.

"It looks like the traumatic force of whatever was used to make this huge lump caused some sort of internal hemorrhaging," one EMT speculated for the cause of the man's death.

"Oh my God!" The manager panicked selfishly thinking about his hotel's reputation as he took a good look at the condition of the room. "Something like this has never happened here!"

"Well, he has no type of identification, so we are gonna need the information of the person who originally rented this room," a policeman interjected so his department could notify the victim's next of kin. "And I'm gonna need to view your surveillance tapes. He didn't hit himself in the head and he damn sure didn't tie himself up!"

Chapter Fourteen

STORM

Although he didn't have his cell phone, Storm woke up automatically knowing time was ticking away on the first balloon payment due date. Four days and counting during one of the worst, if not the worst, times of his life, he stood tall. Waiting for Jordan to come and pick him up, Storm thought about all the things he needed to do. After a quick stop at the Sprint store, followed by solemnly going to the funeral home to make arrangements for O.T., Storm planned for Jordan to stand in for Kenya at the impound lot and get his car released. Hopefully, he'd slip the attendant a couple of dollars, and along with the title, which he had, they'd overlook Jordan not having ID that read Kenya James.

Sitting back in his favorite chair, all he could do was think about the crying sounds of the baby Kenya claimed was his. Unsuccessfully trying to get a hold of London and not having contact information for any of their relatives, Storm was lost. Kenya's cell was also still going to voicemail, so once again out of complete desperation, he reached out to Brother Rasul. Giving him a blow-by-blow description of his and Kenya's conversation, including the baby part, he begged him man to man to help him see his son, if nothing else.

BROTHER RASUL

Brother Rasul left the kitchen to answer the doorbell. At a loss about who it could be, because his associates knew better than to just drop by, he looked through the security peephole. With folded arms and an apparent attitude, Fatima rang the bell once more.

"Yeah." He opened the door not forgetting her disrespecting antics.

"Yeah, I left one of my textbooks, and I need it for class tomorrow."

Brother Rasul knew Kenya was still upstairs in his bed sleeping. Still in bliss from the all-night pussy he'd gotten, he was far from in the mood to explain Kenya's presence, let alone the baby's. He was glad he'd put Kenya's car in the garage to avoid questions from any nosey neighbors and, especially now, Fatima. "Well, wait here. I'll get it. Where'd you leave it at?"

"Umm, I think it's in the den by the couch." Fatima hoped her popping up would give them a chance to make up, but he was still acting hard. "Do you want me to look for it?" She reached for the handle of the iron gate; however, it was locked.

"Naw, I'm good on all that." He pushed the wooden door half shut while he went to locate her supposedly important book.

Fatima couldn't believe his nerve not letting her inside. Standing on the porch, she looked down through the crack in the door and couldn't believe her eyes. *Are those a pair of female shoes near the closet? Oh, no, he ain't got no other female up in there already. I should cut him and that ho!*

When he returned without being able to find the book, Fatima was leaving off the porch done with him for good. She'd quickly come to her senses, knowing she had way too much to lose to be catching a case over dumb shit.

"I couldn't find it," he yelled out the door.

"Forget it. I'm good. But have you spoken to Kenya anymore since the other night?"

"Kenya?" he repeated with guilt in his tone.

Fatima had no idea whatsoever that Kenya was right upstairs in the bed she and Brother Rasul had shared for over a year. "Yeah, I just wanted to know what was going on with London. I keep calling and calling. Her phone is going straight to voicemail. So if you could at least let her know I'm trying to get in contact with her, I'd appreciate it."

Knowing that when Fatima found out her best friend was dead she was going to be devastated, Brother Rasul felt bad, but he had to lie. He had no choice. "I haven't spoken to Kenya since the other night, but I'll try to call her later and check up on London for you."

"Yeah, you do that," Fatima sneered opening her car door. "And tell that slut you got up in there to enjoy my sloppy seconds!"

Allah, I don't mean to question you, for you know what's best. Please guide me.

Knowing what he had to do, Brother Rasul finished making Kenya a light breakfast before he went to work out. The baby was changed and napping. Taking the tray upstairs, he stood at the foot of the bed. There he saw Kenya, still sleeping. He knew what he was feeling was wrong, but after a night of wild, almost anything-goes sex, he was wide open. Far from being a fool, he knew she was still in love with Storm and was only banging him out of revenge, but right about now, he couldn't give a fuck less about her motives.

Sensing him standing over her, Kenya opened her eyes. "Oh, hey," she barely mumbled. "Good morning."

Giving her a chance to use the bathroom and wash her face, Brother Rasul watched her eat while he informed her, rather demanded, that he, she, and Storm's son would be making a road trip back to Dallas in the next few days.

"I'm going to get one of my close pediatrician friends from the mosque to examine the baby, then we good to go."

Of course, Kenya strongly protested, but she eventually gave in. She trusted Brother Rasul's word that he would let no harm come to her, whether it be from Storm or the police.

STORM

Deciding to get an altogether new cell phone number cutting ties from unnecessary people who had the first, including Marco Meriwether, Storm reached in his back pocket taking out his wallet. Finding the card with Anika's number on it, he dialed hoping she'd pick up. When she did, he told her who he was and from this point on if the folk they both worked for needed to get in touch with him, they could do so on the new number he'd just called from.

Considering the way she flirted with him on their ride back from the initial meeting, Storm was a little thrown off at the dryness in her tone. She agreed to deliver the message after offering him her condolences on his younger brother's untimely death. *How did she even know about what happened to O.T.?* His mind puzzled as Jordan drove him to the funeral home.

Maybe it's because she's deep in the street game and immune to losing soldiers or maybe she just isn't a morning person. Whatever the case was, Storm felt Anika's overall coldness throughout the duration of their brief conversation. For a female who was practically throwing the pussy on him a few days ago, she was acting brand new. He wanted to ask her if she thought he could negotiate for another few days on the payment date but could tell in her tone that now wasn't the time.

Besides, even though Jordan seemed preoccupied with something and looked a little bit puffy in the face when she showed up, Storm knew bitches like the back of his hand, and he knew Jordan was still ear-hustling his call. Saying anything about his illegal business dealings in front of some random strip club dancer wanting to get on was completely out the question.

Enduring the sadness of making the final arrangements for his brother, Storm decided since he and O.T. had no real blood relatives to speak of, he'd just have a viewing of the body and then a private ceremony. The director had him sign all the required paperwork and gladly accepted the cash payment from Mr. Tony Christian who he knew was a drug dealer, which made no difference to him. Some of his best clients and paymasters were criminals.

Paying an extra fee for the mortician to rush preparing his brother's body for viewing in the next few days so the entire ordeal could just be over, Storm depressingly left with a clingy Jordan right by his side. Next, they'd go and try to get his car from the impound lot.

Unknown to him, there was a pair of eyes watching his every movement.

Chapter Fifteen

PARIS

"Everything seems so confusing. I can't believe all these months have passed." Paris sat up in the bed still in denial. "The last thing I really can remember is taking a bunch of pills at my apartment."

Kendricks, who'd been forced to take a mandatory leave pending further investigation of Marco Meriwether's escape, had been spending all his free time posted by Paris bedside. Sporting a huge bandage to hide the staples used to close his head wound, he listened attentively, hanging on her every word. Paris was led to believe that the man who was being so helpful was a patient from down the hall, not a policeman fishing for information she may or may not have known.

"Well, you shouldn't push yourself." He turned off his hidden small handheld recorder. "But I did want to tell you something I overheard some of them at the first desk talking about."

Reaching out for Kendricks's hand to help her get into her wheelchair so she could go to physical therapy to regain strength in her leg muscles, Paris was confused. "What are you talking about?"

After getting her safely transferred from the bed, Kendricks inconspicuously turned the recorder back on. Walking over to the table on the far side of the room, he returned with a folded-up newspaper dated a few days prior. "I just thought you should know." Handing her the paper, he stood back so he could study her reaction to the front page headlines.

"Noooo! It can't be! Noooo!" she screamed out not believing the tragic words she'd just read. Throwing the source of her pain to the floor, Paris tried to get up from the wheelchair, but she weakly fell to the ground along-side the newspaper. "Is that why they claim they can't get in touch with anyone from my family? Is it?" she cried. "I don't believe it! Not O.T.! Noooo! Why, Tangy? Why?" Her sobs got louder. "Is that why ain't nobody been here to see about me, not even Kenya?"

Kendricks started to feel bad for the young woman he'd strangely become romantically attached to. He didn't want Paris to suffer, yet the years of him being an officer of the law were motivating him to find out what she knew about Tony "Storm" Christian and his brother, her boyfriend, the now deceased Othello "O.T." Christian. "I guess so." He played dumb. "But why would your cousin kill your boyfriend anyway?"

"Oh, God, what have I been doing? Oh my God!"

She was given a strong sedative by one of the nurses to calm her down, and Kendricks recorded every word Paris mumbled about God giving her another chance to make things right in her tormented life. As a policeman, he was shocked to learn all the crimes she confessed Storm, Kenya, and O.T. had committed and even more shocked to learn the ones she'd personally taken part in herself. *How can somebody so beautiful be so cold,* he wondered, emotionally torn about what to do next with the explosive information he'd just learned.

POLICE
"Kendricks, how you been holding up?" Malloy questioned his partner. "You at home living the life, huh?"

"Naw, man, not really. You know after all this time on the force I miss doing that old-fashioned police work."

"Well, just take this time off to get yourself together. We can make it a few weeks without you. Put your feet up and watch a little television for me. Worrying about the review board ain't gonna make them decide your fate any sooner."

Kendricks, just yards away from Paris's room, held his cell up to his ear listening to the advice of his old friend and comrade. Leaning against the wall, tape recorder in hand, he informed Malloy that he wanted to meet up with him later. "Listen up, guy. I done stumbled up on some information that I know is gonna make the review board just about build a statue in my honor."

Excited at the thought, Malloy eagerly agreed. Before ending their conversation, he gave Kendricks an update on the leads the department was following up on. "Make it first thing in the morning. Today is gonna be a long one. It seems as if Marco Meriwether's prints were found at a crime scene at a hotel."

"Oh, yeah?" Kendricks snarled angry at himself for dropping the ball letting that animal back on the streets. "What kind of scene was it?"

Malloy knew how Kendricks was feeling, but he told him the truth just the same. "Homicide. The victim this time was a plastic surgeon. I just got finished trying to calm the man's distraught wife down. She was beyond hysterical. For her privacy and the sake of the department, we're keeping his murder real low-key. Oh, yeah, there was another set of prints on the scene besides Marco's, but they weren't in the system. We still going through tapes and questioning the hotel staff."

The suspended officer had enough. "I'll just see you in the a.m." Kendricks shut his cell and went back to sit by Paris's side.

MARCO

Marco continued following Jordan. Her every movement, he was there. First out to Storm's condo, then to the Sprint store, and finally to the funeral home, he was on her trail. In between answering calls from Big Doc B's wife, begging for a reason for her husband's murder, calls from the wannabe-tough cop Malloy, urging him to turn himself in, and texting Jordan that he was gonna fuck her up if she tried to cross him again, Marco plotted his next move in making sure Storm suffered for all the threats, insults, and inconvenience he'd caused him. He knew deep down, he should've just been trying to get out of town, but now he was banging on point and principle.

So this is where that good shit-talking O.T.'s hookup gonna be at? Marco hissed turning down the car's sound system. "I should show up and spit in that nigga's face while he lying on display or at least shoot the son of a bitch service up. Or maybe I should just rush up in there now and kill everybody!"

Parking half a block down, so he could still see the funeral home entrance and Jordan's car, he went through Doc's glove compartment and middle console to pass the time. Luckily, he discovered some bacterial ointment in Doc's ever-present medical bag to soothe the still-burning feeling of the deep scratches Jordan made on his face. Feeling like he'd hit the lottery, he then pocketed some bottles of pills.

Just short of an hour later, high off some of the prescription drugs, he saw Storm and Jordan exit the building and pull off. Driving at least three cars behind, he saw them go through the gate of the city impound lot.

"Oh, shit, this is perfect." High as a kite, he got out of the BMW tossing the keys on the passenger seat.

Back in the day, Marco and his crew used to steal cars off this very lot and joyride for days before the owners, who finally scraped up enough money to retrieve their automobiles, or the employees even knew the vehicles were missing from the premises. Slipping through the same flimsy fence near the rear corner of the lot, Marco picked a Chrysler minivan. Chrysler ignitions were always the easiest to break down. Five minutes later, with the aid of a piece of metal he'd torn off another car's front grill, the van was started, and he was plowing recklessly through the fence and out of the general area.

"It ain't no need to follow them bitches anymore. I know where they laying they heads at!" Marco laughed blasting the factory radio. "Besides, I got unfinished business at the hospital to take care of."

Removing the battery after disabling the GPS, he felt somewhat at ease. Creeping up in the hospital parking lot, Marco used the minute TracFone he'd just purchased from a corner store. After abandoning Doc's BMW, he knew it would only be a matter of time before the police started trying to get hits off of different cell phone towers and try to pinpoint his general location if he kept using Doc's cell; however, he needed all the contact numbers in the phone, so he pocketed it. Calling the front desk of the hospital, he asked for Nurse Jamison. Marco hung up instantly when she picked up.

Good, that bitch at work. Reclining the driver's seat of the stolen minivan, he sat back waiting for Jordan's sister to get off her shift. Licking his lips, he smiled. *I'ma get some of that goody-goody stuck-up pussy tonight! I hope she's a freak like her sister.*

Chapter Sixteen

STORM

Storm woke up with constant thoughts of London stuck in his mind. Relentlessly trying to get in touch with his baby momma was getting him no closer to finding out if what Kenya's malicious ass said was indeed true, that London did have the baby and was choosing not to be bothered with him.

"Naw, London wouldn't do anything like that," Storm reasoned out loud as his phone started to vibrate. "But right about now, I ain't got time to worry about it. I need to focus on my brother and paying that damn money back on time. These fellas don't play." He pushed the envelope button showing that Anika must've passed on his new cell number. "I know, I know. Three days. Damn, I'm working on it!"

After taking a long, hot shower, Storm went downstairs to find Ponytail just coming back inside from feeding his dog, and Jordan sitting on the couch in tears. "Shit, what the fuck is wrong with you? What's with all the tears? Was the mattress in the spare room that hard?"

Ponytail stepped in answering the question for Jordan, who seemed much too upset to speak, let alone laugh at Storm trying to be funny. "Man, somebody just called and told her that her sister was in the emergency room."

"The emergency room?" Storm had enough of hospitals for a lifetime, and it showed by his facial expression. "Why? What happened?"

Ponytail waited to see if Jordan was going to answer this time. When she didn't, he pulled Storm over to the other side of the living room. "From what I could get out of her, in between the tears, her older sister was beaten, raped, and left for dead. They found her behind some office building across town."

Storm felt bad he'd been monopolizing all of Jordan's time. Time she probably should have been spending with her own family. Putting his arms around her in hopes of easing her pain, Storm asked Jordan if there was anything that he or Ponytail could do, including riding with her to the hospital.

"Naw, I'm good. My other family is down there," she lied knowing it was just her and her sister living in town. "I really don't get along with my people. They don't like what I do for a living, so they kinda don't deal with me or want me anywhere around."

Her fake tears should've won her an Academy Award or a Daytime Emmy. Jordan could truly not care less about her sister being brutally attacked and left for dead. If anything, after the way she ignored Marco's calls the entire evening, she kinda expected it. She'd ignored his calls all night, so she assumed this was his way of sending a message that he wasn't bullshitting around with her anymore.

"Yo, I know how that shit goes." Storm sucked his teeth thinking about being alone in the world now that his brother was gone.

"Yeah, that's pretty messed up," Ponytail agreed nodding his head to the side.

Storm caught on realizing his boy wanted to talk to him about something in private. Considering he didn't want to let Jordan's good ear-hustling self in on his business, he and Ponytail walked toward the rear of the kitchen, past the walk-in freezer door where London's body still lay behind. Not being able to talk because of Reckless's loud barks, they stepped out in the backyard to speak in private.

Once outside, Storm was informed that while they were sleep, apparently an out-of-control Marco had robbed two of their spots. Furious, Storm was about to explode when he found out the amount of cash and product that was stolen.

"Out of all the times to take a fucking hit, this is the damn worst!" He knocked over the barbeque pit and kicked a hole through the wooden fence separating him and his nosey elderly neighbor, Mrs. Farrow. "We need to try to make that grip up. And how in the hell did that goofy fool Marco catch them young boys slipping? I need to just suit up and hunt that buster down my-damn-self!"

Ponytail put his hand on Storm's shoulder reassuring him that he was gonna grind extra hard the next two days. "For real, man, don't worry. I'ma make it do what it do, besides I gotta come up with some extra ends to shoot to my girl. She been blowing my cell up, bugging. And as for Marco, after you deal with your brother, if his stupid ass is still fool enough to be lingering around, I'll suit up with you!"

"That's what's up," Storm agreed as they pounded fists.

JORDAN

Making sure Storm and Ponytail were out of her eyesight, Jordan ran over to the kitchen window peeping through the curtain. With the dog barking like he had lost his mind, she tiptoed back into the living room. Hitting the redial button, she returned one of Marco's numerous calls from a random cell. Two rings in, he picked up.

"Yeah, bitch, so now you wanna call a nigga, huh? You over there playing house with that pretty boy! Well, both of y'all can suck my dick and oh, yeah, tell him I said thanks for the extra dough." Marco lay in the rear of the van he'd slept in, counting the stolen money from Storm's dope houses.

"Oh, so I see you been real busy, huh?" Jordan sarcastically replied. "But all that flapping your gums don't mean a damn thang. The cops gonna catch up with you sooner or later."

Marco smiled. "Well, when that day come, it just fucking comes. And by the way, your sister pussy is way more better than yours and tighter. I choked the bitch to death with this hard pipe! I'ma true pimp!"

"Death." Jordan snickered while making sure Storm and his boy weren't back inside the condo yet. "Look, you half-ass motherfucker, FYI, my sister is still alive. The hospital just called me, but if she do end up dying, then I'm the one who's gonna get blessed with a big, fat life insurance check. So your dumb ass did me a favor!" Jordan brazenly got off into Marco's shit. "So tell me who's the true pimp now!"

Marco was infuriated. "If you do fuck around and got some revenue coming, I swear to God you ain't gonna get a chance to spend it! So fuck you!"

"Naw, faggot, trust. Fuck you!" Jordan, feeling safe staying in Storm's condo, hung up hearing the fellas coming back in through the kitchen door.

With Ponytail out in the streets getting that bread, Storm and Jordan spent the day going through his closet to find the perfect outfit for the funeral director to dress O.T. in. Temporarily putting a smile on Storm's face, Jordan sat on the edge of his bed going back down memory lane. Reminiscing about the many nights he, she, O.T., and even Deacon spent up in Alley Cats getting lifted after they closed, Storm wished he could turn back the hands of time. Jordan reminded him of all the good times they shared and even some not so good.

Although he always thought Jordan was cute in her own way, he never had any romantic feelings for her. Yet, all in all, it felt great to have someone, other than his boy Ponytail, to kick it with about his loss.

Jordan, not thinking anymore about the tragic attack on her innocent sister initiated by her involvement with Marco, sat back waiting and hoping for the chance to bang Storm's brains out. She wanted to ask him about Kenya and dry snitch she'd found out his wifey was fucking Big Doc B and the baby she was carrying could possibly be Doc's, but Jordan knew the last time she tried even mentioning Kenya's name, Storm went bananas.

Besides, how would she explain how she found out from jump? She damn straight couldn't say Marco showed her the video. Jordan's best bet was to keep quiet and imagine how she was gonna redecorate Storm's condo. And that's just what she did.

Chapter Seventeen

BROTHER RASUL/ KENYA

It was early Wednesday morning. With a full tank of gas, Brother Rasul, who was all in physically and mentally for Kenya, turned his truck out of the service station heading toward the interstate. Safe and sound, the small infant, Li'l Stone, was strapped in his car seat. Kenya, his aunt, was lying back in the passenger seat, still nervous about returning to Storm and Dallas. She knew Brother Rasul had power in Detroit, but Dallas was clear across the map. She didn't know how Storm was gonna react to seeing her, his newborn son, or London who was, as far as she knew, still in his walk-in freezer.

As they started their long journey, Kenya closed her eyes getting chills as she went down the long laundry list of the crimes she'd committed or been a part of the past year including murder, extortion, racketeering, fraud, assault, receiving stolen property, transporting drugs, manufacturing of drugs and, the worst crime of all, if not legally, then certainly morally, which was standing idly by watching her sister die.

I guess Brother Rasul is right. I do need to go back and straighten things out, at least with Storm. And damn, London do deserve better, I guess. But how she think it was all right to have a baby by my man? Brought out of her daydream by a gigantic pothole and her cell phone vibration, Kenya got herself emotionally prepared to listen to both her and London's messages as they rode.

STORM

Waking up heated, Storm wanted nothing more than to speak with London. Although Kenya was being a class A bitch, he knew London would at least be honest with him if she'd indeed given birth to his son. After trying to call London, saying, "Can you please call me?" he lastly dialed Kenya, leaving the message, "Bitch, I done told you to run my money!" Less than five minutes later, like clockwork, he received a text from the connect: 2.

Storm was frustrated, regretting he'd even made the drug deal in the first place. Everything that could go wrong in his once perfect world had. Hollering downstairs for Jordan to come up, he packed the garment bag she was going to drop off at the funeral home. O.T.'s body would be ready for viewing the next day if she got the clothes to them no later than noon, so that was the plan.

Lending her his car, which they'd successfully gotten out of impound, Storm told her a few of his favorites to pick up from the grocery store on her way back. Jordan wanted to cook both of them dinner the night before, but either of them going to see what food was stored inside the walk-in freezer was definitely out of the question. Reckless would start barking for hours on end. And with Ponytail out all night hustling not being able to calm the vicious albino pit bull down, they just ordered a small pizza and two rib tip dinners to be delivered.

When Jordan left, Storm started the long task of calling every single guy he'd ever done business with to try either to collect money they previously owed him or to offer to sell them some top-notch uncut product at a fair rate. He knew the chances of him getting the cash back from Kenya were slim to none. Ponytail was doing his part to meet the deadline; now it was time for him to temporarily stop mourning O.T. and do the same. Storm knew that in less than twenty-four hours from now, his cell would show the number 1, and he'd be getting texted instructions on where to make the first money drop.

JORDAN

"Thank you, miss." The greedy, sometimes unscrupulous funeral director took the bag briefly examining the contents. "You can tell Mr. Christian his brother's body will definitely be ready first thing in the morning. I have my best people on top of it."

"Okay, I will." Jordan turned to walk away as he instinctively looked at her wide backside.

Almost three times her age, being a man, he still flirted. "Umm, miss, just wondering. Exactly what is your relationship to the deceased?"

Jordan had a devilish grin on her face, the kind the funeral director often saw when it was discovered one mournful family member was being more financially blessed with the passing of a loved one than the next. Besides Christmas and income tax refund time, a person dying and leaving you a li'l something somethin' were the best times in a black person's life. Being the beneficiary was like winning the lottery and Jordan looked like she'd just hit the Powerball.

"My name is Jordan. Let's just say I'm a real, real close friend of the family." She winked before leaving the older man lusting.

Driving Storm's car, Jordan felt like she was on top of the world. Feeling a small bit of sympathy for her sister, she then decided to take time out of her busy schedule of trying to wedge herself into Storm's life and check on her sibling, Nurse Jamison. After seeing her battered and bruised, black and blue with a feeding tube in her mouth, Jordan felt a small bit of remorse for what Marco had done, but not enough to stay more than ten minutes at her often judgmental sister's bedside.

After swinging by the market grabbing the items on Storm's list, Jordan couldn't help herself. She had to floss. Whipping up in the parking lot of one of the grimiest projects in town, Jordan phoned one of her girlfriends to come out and see her whipping Storm's ride. Bragging that she was staying with him out at his condo and that bitch from Detroit Kenya was out of the picture, Jordan was feeling herself for real.

"Yeah, you see I got those groceries in the back seat. Let me bounce; a bitch gotta get back to the new crib and tend to my new man," Jordan bragged as she exaggerated her new status in Storm's life.

Making one last tour of the hood showing off, Jordan was unaware Marco, brazenly out on the prowl, had spotted her. Caught up in her own self-indulgent world, she turned up the music heading back to the suburban condo as Marco, cracking his knuckles, then rubbing the still painful scratches on his face trailed five cars behind.

MARCO

"Oh, this ho think she fancy, huh?" Marco shrugged his shoulders, spotting Jordan driving one of Storm's cars through the neighborhood. "Good. She out acting like a nigga can't reach out and touch that hot ass. As soon as she slips, she good as dead!"

Marco, not worried about getting recaptured, followed her every move. Realizing the direction Jordan was now heading, he knew her time flossing must have been just about up. Easing his hand over to the passenger seat, he picked up his gun. "When this ho slow down, I'ma light that motherfucker up!" Several cars turned off, leaving only one vehicle in between him and Jordan. Seconds before he was gonna make his move, Jordan turned into a 7-Eleven. *Damn, ain't this some shit!* Marco thought as he frowned, staring dead at two police cruisers.

Luckily for Jordan, both cops were preoccupied trying to sort out what seemed like a small group of teens who'd been caught shoplifting; otherwise, Marco would've had one more body added to his ever-growing list and Jordan would've been laid out in the funeral home right next to O.T. In the midst of the 7-Eleven chaotic confusion, Jordan pranced out with a huge cherry Big Gulp Slurpee in her hands not paying attention to the cops, the teens, or the store manager who was going ham. Backing out of the small parking lot hitting the road again, Jordan didn't even notice the minivan Marco was driving pull off from the side of the road. As four cars separated them, Marco grew inpatient watching Jordan finally turn off on Storm's block.

JORDAN

Slowly trailing behind a silver older-model Ford, Jordan, extra careful not wanting to spill any, placed her Slurpee in the cup holder. Laying on her car horn, she tried repeatedly to go around the extremely slow driver, but she was having no luck. Turning the tree-lined corner, Jordan was relieved she was almost back to the condo. *Why in the fuck do they still let these old people have licenses?* she wondered when the slow-moving Ford pulled into the driveway directly next to Storm's and an elderly white woman got out.

"Didn't you hear me blowing my horn?" Jordan disrespectfully yelled across the small patch of grass. "I was even flashing my lights! That means get over!"

"Excuse me, dear, but what's the big rush?" Mrs. Farrow questioned barely making it on her cane. After a long morning of running errands, including also going to the market and pharmacy to pick up her heart medicine, she was quick to pass judgment on Jordan and all younger people in general. "You young generation are always moving so fast."

Jordan started taking the bags of groceries out of the rear seat of Storm's expensive sports car mumbling insults at the older woman under her breath the entire time. "Just shut up already, okay? Damn!" were Jordan's final words to Mrs. Farrow who struggled to get even the first of her five bags of groceries out of her trunk while holding on to her handbag and cane.

No sooner than Storm unlocked the front door for Jordan, she disappeared behind the walls of the condo out of the eyesight of both Mrs. Farrow as well as an infuriated Marco, who was hell-bent on killing the bitch.

MARCO

Parking the stolen minivan at the very end of the block, Marco had all intentions of rushing up on Jordan and gunning her down in broad daylight. At this point, in between her smart-ass mouth and attitude thinking she was bigger than the game, he didn't give a shit who saw him. As long as Jordan was dead, also Storm, he'd be content living the rest of his days locked behind bars if he was caught.

Not making it down the block in enough time to catch Jordan before she went in the house, Marco's sudden presence startled old Mrs. Farrow.

"Oh, young man, where did you come from?" she asked with a bag containing bread and eggs dangling from her shaky arm. "I don't think I know you."

"Umm, naw, you don't." Marco pulled his shirt down making sure he hid the handle of his pistol. "But I saw you needed help with these bags," he quickly responded taking the rest of her bags out of her car's trunk.

Mrs. Farrow was happy to see at least one of the younger folk would help the elderly out. "Well, thank you. You must be friends of Mr. Christian and that other nice girl, Kenya. Where has she been anyway?" she pryingly quizzed going toward her front door then unlocking it.

"Do you know anything about that brother of his funeral? Are you a relative?" she assumed because Marco was black. "You know it was in my driveway, don't you? This section of town used to be so quiet. You people are . . ."

Nonchalantly muttering her racist backhanded comments about her neighbors, Marco got his next big idea formulating in his mind. *This old white KKK bitch think I'm cool with Storm's punk ass just because I'm a nigger. Stankin' Bengay-smelling ass!* Without a second thought, Marco shoved the elderly woman through her doorway and onto the floor of her living room. Her pale white skin turned instantly beet red as she grabbed her chest. Marco calmly shut the door of Mrs. Farrow's condo behind him and idly stood by as she suffered a major heart attack from being frightened. *Oh, hell naw, I done scared this lady to death.*

Chapter Eighteen

BROTHER RASUL/KENYA

Having driven what seemed like nonstop, Brother Rasul, Kenya, and the baby finally arrived in Dallas. Still apprehensive about what was gonna happen when she and Storm came face to face, Kenya agreed with Brother Rasul when he suggested getting a room so they could all three get cleaned up. With mixed emotions, especially considering the various messages Storm had left for her and her sister, Kenya's heart raced. Kenya found out from one message in particular that her best friend Paris, who she'd even killed Chocolate Bunny for, was out of her trance and asking for friends and family members. Kenya wished she could call her or go out to the facility so they could figure out what she should do next about Storm and her sister's death, but that was out of the question.

Making sure London would receive a proper burial and Storm could see his son were the only things on her and Brother Rasul's short list to accomplish while they were in town. After that, it was back home to Detroit. That was unless she and Storm could work things out. However, that option was not included in Brother Rasul's overall game plan, but Kenya was strangely still open for whatever, despite all the bullshit that'd jumped off, especially now that London was out of the way.

Two hours later, Brother Rasul turned into the funeral home where he'd found out from his people that O.T.'s body was lying in rest. Going around to the passenger seat, like a gentleman, he opened the door for Kenya before taking the infant car seat out the rear. Entering the often tearful establishment, Brother Rasul kept Li'l Stone with him as Kenya slowly approached the small chapel viewing room off to the side. In tears, she stood beside the brass, polished casket looking down at the man who was her brother-in-law for the past year.

Reaching for some tissue, Kenya wiped her eyes, sad his life had ended so soon. She knew Tangy, and he had a violent history with one another, but not to the point of murder. Reliving the good times in her mind, she also grieved for London. She was lost in her thoughts, and soon another female joined her in the chapel. Not saying a word to her, Kenya quietly signed her name to the guest book, leaving the girl, who was probably one of O.T.'s many "special friends," to mourn in privacy.

"Are you good?" Brother Rasul asked coming out of the funeral director's office. "Is everything okay?"

"Yeah, I'm okay." Kenya wiped her eyes once more. "I just hate seeing O.T. like that."

The funeral director responded to Kenya like he did to everyone grieving. "It's always a sad time when we lose a loved one. But just know we are here for you in your time of need." Shaking Brother Rasul's hand reassuring him he would definitely be able to handle the business they'd just discussed, he was overjoyed when his next appointment, an older well-dressed woman, came inside the lobby, meaning even more revenue for his pockets.

Heading out the door, Brother Rasul went out first with the baby, while Kenya got a free calendar off the table. Wiping her eyes once more, she bumped into the lady. "I'm so sorry." Kenya held the calendar close to her breast looking the woman in her eyes. "I wasn't paying attention. I'm sorry."

The older woman, obviously upset in her own right, didn't say a word. She just stared, glassy-eyed at Kenya as she walked to the truck.

When Kenya got inside the truck, Brother Rasul informed her that the shady-dealing mortician would be able to ship London's body back to Detroit. Also, he would be able to get them a fraudulent death certificate. Giving the man a couple of thousand for his trouble on top of the general undertaker fee easily made one of their huge problems go away. Now the only thing was to go by Storm's and transport the body back to the funeral home themselves. Of course, while they were there Kenya and Storm could make peace and figure out what to do next about his son, her nephew.

STORM

After a solid week of suffering through one of the worst times of his life, Storm awoke with a hangover big enough for three men to split. Squinting his eyes, he snatched at the sheet and was speechless when Jordan pulled back.

"What in the fuck?" Storm jumped up. Forgetting about his pounding headache and the urge to throw up the dinner Jordan half-ass cooked for him the night prior, he yelled. "Yo, Jordan, yo, wake up. What you think you doing?"

Truthfully Jordan had been wide awake at least a good hour or so. After years of wanting to open her eyes to see Storm sleeping next to her, she wanted to make the time stretch out and last forever. "Hmm, what's going on, babe?" she cooed trying to sound sexy.

Storm, completely naked, had no shame as he stood there, dick hard as a rock saluting. "Jordan, why you up here? Didn't I tell you that you could crash on the couch downstairs or the guestroom if you wanted to stay?"

Getting on her knees, Jordan seductively crawled across the king-sized bed. Face to face with Storm's manhood, she stared up into his eyes. "Why you tripping? You told me to come sleep with you. You told me you wanted this pussy." She reached back touching herself. "I only did what you asked me to do. Remember, right after Ponytail dropped off that money and that bottle of Rémy?"

Storm was confused about what he'd said, let alone done the night before. Despite what he and Kenya were going through, banging Jordan was the last thing he wanted to do. Sure, she'd been helpful as a motherfucker, but as soon as the ticket money was paid, he was gonna look out. Feeling the heat of Jordan's hot morning breath on his dick's head, Storm was moments from giving into temptation when his cell phone rang. "Yeah, hello?" He backed away from the bedside going into the bathroom.

"Yes, Mr. Christian. This is the funeral director. I just wanted you to know we worked extra hard and long all night." He smooth-talked him, hoping for another tip from his assumed drug dealer client.

"And?"

"And your brother's body is ready for viewing. Matter of fact, since we've been open, there's already been a few mourners here."

"Oh, yeah." Storm used his shoulder to hold the cell to his ear as he pissed. "Who were they this damn early?"

The funeral director looked at the clock on his wall. Although it was regular business hours for most, he forgot that folks in the drug game often set their own hours. "They signed the family book we complimentary provided. We'll speak later when you get here about any other things you might need. Now you must excuse me, a grieving widow needs my attention."

Before putting on some clothes, Storm looked at his phone's screen noticing that the number 1 had been sent via text almost an hour ago with a location and a time for the payment drop off. *Damn, I must've been knocked the hell out for real. I usually hear this motherfucker.* Glad Jordan was out of his bed when he came from the bathroom, Storm decided after the funeral service was over the next day, he'd tell her she had to leave. There was no real point in making Jordan think that she could ever be his wifey. Even if he never heard from Kenya again in life, Storm knew Jordan was nothing but a trick and a whore, definitely not wifey material.

Going downstairs, Storm was met by Ponytail, worn out and exhausted coming through the front door, and Jordan in the kitchen calling herself trying to cook brunch.

"Hey, dude, what it do?"

"Hey, Storm, what's up, guy?" He reached in both his pockets pulling out knots. "This is from the last four hours from the three spots that's still pumping."

"Whoa, good looking, Ponytail. I appreciate it. Today is that day. Plus that greedy old dude at the funeral home said they got my brother all proper looking, you feel me?"

"That's what's up." Ponytail wanted to feed Reckless before going to his house to try to patch things up with his girl, but he wasn't in the mood for Jordan to be in there tripping. "I'ma swing by there later to pay my respects. I need to kick it with my kids first, then get some rest."

When Ponytail left, Storm went back upstairs deliberately ignoring Jordan and staying focusing on counting his money. After the week-long grind, Storm was still a little over $5,000 short. He'd collected debts from everyone, Ponytail stayed in the streets hustling, he'd slashed his regular weight prices, and he'd even pawned a few items Kenya hadn't taken. But he was still a little light on the ticket. If it weren't for her stealing his money or Marco robbing his spots or worst of all having to cash out for O.T.'s funeral service, Storm would've had it all.

Five Gs short outta a $40,000 ticket ain't all that bad. I'll get it to them in a few days and they'll be straight. Shit, a thirty-five G run in a week after all the bullshit I've been through? Where the fuck they do that at? Storm, telling Jordan he'd be back later in the evening, left to make the drop at the texted location, then get his hair cut before going to the funeral home.

Within eighteen minutes of leaving the house, the drop was made and he felt somewhat relieved. Trying to call Anika's cell and inform her he was a little bit short and would make it up, Storm was sent to voicemail. Leaving a message for her to get back at him, he drove to the barber shop, which was a few blocks over from the funeral home. After a fresh cut and lineup, Storm solemnly sat in the parking lot of the funeral home trying to get the courage to go inside the building. The thought of seeing his brother cold, stiff, and lifeless was more than he could stand. Storm didn't care who was walking by or who would be in there. Really, for the first time since he'd broken down at the hospital, Storm openly sobbed, struggling to come to terms that his brother and best friend was truly gone, never coming back.

JORDAN
"It don't matter he was too drunk to fuck last night; he still gonna be my man and one day my baby daddy," Jordan said out loud over the dog's constant barking. "He can be in denial all he want to, but I know he want all of this." She stirred a pot of ghetto chili she called herself making for their dinner.

Leaving it to simmer, as soon as Ponytail and finally Storm had both left the condo, she turned on the radio and went upstairs. Despite his reaction to waking up finding her in his bed, Jordan knew Storm would be a fool not to be with her. Straightening up the mess that Kenya obviously had made days ago before leaving, Jordan unpacked her bag, hanging up her clothes in Kenya's closet. In between each item she hung up, Marco kept calling her cell talking cash shit, like he'd been doing all the evening before and half the night.

At one point during her and Storm getting buzzed, he joked all those harassing calls must be Big Doc B trying to get at her. Stunned he knew about her and Doc's arrangement, Jordan wanted to reveal the scandalous shit she knew about Doc and Kenya and see how funny Storm thought that conversation was.

Ready to just take a steaming hot shower and relax in her new surroundings, Jordan answered Marco's call one last time before vowing to get her number changed by Sprint.

"What!"

"Bitch, I'ma get your ass real, real soon. Trust. Be patient. I'ma kill you first then Storm!"

"Stop calling me, loser. You need to be getting the fuck out of town before they catch your dumb ass and lock you up in a cage like the animal you are."

"You think because you up in that faggot's crib you some sort of boss!" Marco hissed searching through old Mrs. Farrow's belongings. "Well, I saw his punk ass leave and when you go visit your sister—"

"My sister," she taunted. "Boy, bye, fuck her and you. I'm over that! And so what Storm left? He'll be back crying about his dead brother and all up in this pussy! You can kick rocks and do what you gotta do! I'm out!" Stripping down Jordan stepped into the shower. *I ain't bullshitting. I gotta call Sprint!*

Chapter Nineteen

BROTHER RASUL/ KENYA

A nervous wreck, Kenya's palms sweated and her hands shook as she instructed Brother Rasul to turn the corner of the block she and Storm had been living on for the past year. When he reached the driveway she pointed out, he pulled in.

"Okay, this is it. I don't know whose car that is," Kenya motioned to the candy apple red Toyota belonging to Jordan sitting in front of the condo. "Maybe it's one of nosey Mrs. Farrow's kids who hardly come to visit her."

Brother Rasul looked up toward each end of the street trying to figure out how he could get London's body loaded into the rear of his truck without the neighbors suspecting anything. "Hey, Kenya, I was wondering—"

"I already know." Glancing back at the sleeping baby, Kenya got out of the truck, praying Storm wasn't at home. That way at least they'd get a chance to get London out of there without added controversy. Walking over to the electronic keypad located on the side, Kenya punched in the security code causing the attached garage door to open wide. "Thank God he ain't here. Come on, pull inside, and leave the baby in there. He asleep anyhow."

Brother Rasul and Kenya went through the always unlocked door directly into the side entrance of the condo. Met by the sounds of music and the smells of something cooking, both he and Kenya were confused.

"I thought no one was at home."

"Storm's car isn't here. Maybe he just left the radio playing," Kenya speculated walking over the area of the living room floor she'd let London die on. "And I don't know why he left this pot on. His ass don't even cook." Leading him into the kitchen, they soon heard a dog start barking. Scared, Kenya reached back for Brother Rasul's arm.

"It's a dog, Kenya," he said, trying to ease her fears. "I didn't know y'all had a dog."

"Yeah, neither did I," Kenya replied feeling like she was in a foreign place not somewhere that up until a week ago she called home. "But if you can go back there, my sister's body is behind that second door. Can you just get her? I can't see her like that anymore."

Leaving Brother Rasul to clean up her dirty work, Kenya headed up the stairs to get a few more of her personal belongings she'd left behind. With each step, something just didn't seem right. First the pot on the stove, then the dog barking, and now she smelled the aroma of her cucumber melon body wash. *What the fuck?* Entering the master bedroom, Kenya heard sounds coming from the shower in her bathroom. The closer she got, she could see the steam slipping through the semi-closed door. *Who in the hell?*

Slowly pushing the door open, Kenya discovered that there was a person inside her private domain. Not knowing what to think, instinctively Kenya armed herself with a family-size bottle of bleach she kept underneath the sink. *I'ma blind me a motherfucker real quick!* Twisting the cap off, she braced up. Moving quietly toward the glass shower door there was about to be sheer hell to be paid. Seconds before she raised her hand to pull the handle, the water suddenly stopped. Not wanting to give whoever the opportunity to be prepared, hood-wise Kenya flung the door open splashing bleach everywhere.

"Oh my God, argggg," Jordan painfully screamed out from the surprise attack. "I can't see, arggg, it's burning, arggg! My eyes, my fucking eyes." Her arms, which had bleach on them as well, swung wildly trying to find the knob to turn back on the water and hopefully wash off the chemical that was poisonous to the skin. "Help me! Urggg, it's burning! Oh my God!"

"Jordan! Oh, hell naw. Jordan?" Kenya immediately recognized her ex-employee from Alley Cats. "Why in the fuck is you at my damn house, in my fucking shower? Have you lost your entire mind? What the fuck is going on?"

"Is that you, Kenya?" Jordan was relieved, thinking that somehow Marco had gotten inside the condo and made good on his promise to get at her. "Kenya, please help me. Whatever that was is burning my skin like a motherfucker and I can't see! Please, girl," she continued to beg as Kenya stood idly by.

Setting the almost empty plastic bottle on the sink, it was about to get real. Preparing herself to do real battle, Kenya went aggressively in. "Bitch, didn't I ask you what the fuck you doing at my goddamn house? Your ass might be burning but you ain't deaf, you heard me? And where the fuck is Storm?"

"Kenya, damn, please," Jordan begged, hoping for a miracle and some sort of grace from her old boss.

Jordan frantically moved her hands along the moist, sweating walls. Her heart raced as the burning feeling intensified. Finally, she found the knob and attempted to turn it on.

Not in the mood for any games or further delays, Kenya was not playing around. She wanted answers. Some random ho suffering bleach burns in her shower didn't mean jack shit to her. Using her foot, she kicked a naked, dripping wet Jordan dead in the stomach causing her to fall in the corner of the marble floor. Not letting up or feeling any sort of sympathy, Kenya stumped her out. Combined with the rage she'd been feeling all week from London's senseless death, O.T.'s untimely murder, Storm's deceitful betrayal, and having to drive all the way to Detroit, then back, a grown man couldn't stand a chance to win against her right about now, let alone a naked trick with bleach tears in her eyes.

"Okay, Jordan, you ready to answer my questions or you want me to really burn that ass? It's up to you 'cause I don't give a dry fuck." Kenya reached back toward the sink for the bottle.

"Wait, Kenya, damn, wait." Jordan couldn't see clearly, but she knew Kenya was moving ready to back up her threats.

Finally feeling like she was going to try to explain, Kenya turned on the cold water. "I wanna hear this bullshit. But trust no matter what in the fuck you say, you damn straight getting another ass kicking before you leave!"

Allowing the cold water to flush her eyes out and her body off, Jordan crawled into the other corner of the shower trying to catch her breath. Being able to make out Kenya's shadow, Jordan knew she needed medical treatment immediately if she hoped to see properly in the future. "Kenya, please, it's still burning."

Not feeling any remorse, Kenya coldly stared into Jordan's beet red, swollen eyes demanding an explanation one more time before she promised to kill her. "Look, bitch, this ain't a joke okay? Now, this is the last fucking time I'ma ask you. Why in the fuck is you here? I know Storm ain't fucking your skank ass. If you tell me that, you and him both gonna die!"

Panting for air, Jordan swore that she and Storm hadn't fucked. And in reality, she was telling the truth. In between begging for more cold water and rubbing at her irritated eyes, she informed her that Storm was gone to view O.T.'s body. She explained to Kenya that her and his homeboy Ponytail had been staying there to keep Storm company. "It ain't like what you think, Kenya, I swear on everything I love. Storm ain't been checking for me. It's not like that." Jordan ran her con game down praying it worked. "We just been here because Storm been nutting up. We just been having his back while you was gone that's all. Storm said I could use this shower. I swear I ain't mean no disrespect to you. I swear."

"You and Ponytail?" Kenya recognized his name as one of Storm's boys from back in the day and she kind of eased up on her rage.

Jordan picked up on the fact that Kenya thought she and Ponytail were really a couple and she ran with it. "Yeah, me and him been here just trying to keep your man from going crazy, just kicking it. Where you been anyway?" She tried flipping the script hoping for mercy.

"What?" Kenya was thrown off at the question and didn't know what to say.

"Is y'all two beefing hard behind that Big Doc B bullshit or what?"

Kenya was stunned she'd even mentioned Doc. "Hold up, bitch, what in the entire hell you talking about?"

At that point, Jordan knew the tables were about to turn, and she monopolized on it. "Listen, girl, I've been banging him too, but I ain't tripping. He is a good paymaster. It ain't no thang. He everybody cash cow from down at the club."

"Banging him? Who, Doc? Why you say that stupid shit?" Kenya didn't know what to say next or what to do. *I know Doc's ass ain't tell this good gossiping bitch what happened. I swear if he did that dumb shit . . .*

After getting Kenya to turn back on the water, Jordan finally stood to her feet. She rinsed the still-burning chemical off her skin the best she could before Kenya's mercy wore off. Stepping out the shower, buck-naked and soaking wet, the stripper had no shame, not even asking for a towel. Delusional in her thoughts, she wanted Kenya to see what she was working with and what Storm was gonna be getting every night when she got rid of her Detroit ass once and for all. Pretending that Doc, not Marco, had shown her and a few other people the infamous video, Jordan saw the horror plastered on Kenya's otherwise smug face. "Yeah, girl, a bunch of us seen it. I ain't gonna lie, you got a hellava head game." Jordan gave her a half-cocked smile. "Storm is one lucky man. Shit, I wish you liked to eat pussy like you suck dick. I'd definitely be down."

"Storm." Kenya felt dizzy thinking about the video she'd made only to ensure Doc's silence about the baby, not for him to show every random ho in town. "I gotta go." She suddenly turned around gathering up a few items and stuffing them into a bag. "Damn, I gotta go," she mumbled once again while Jordan took the opportunity to splash more water from the sink in her eyes.

"Don't worry, girl, Storm is so fucked up behind O.T., I don't think he has time to worry about you and the next man who getting his wet wet," Jordan remarked raising up with water dripping from her face. "And dang, what's going on with the baby? That shit crazy as hell."

Pausing at the doorway, Kenya couldn't believe her ears. *Hold up, this bitch even know about the baby? I wonder did she see my sister down there too?* "What you mean baby?"

"I saw all the baby stuff in the other room, so I figured—"

"Figured what?" Kenya waited to hear what Jordan was gonna say next determining if she had to kill her as well.

"Well, when you weren't here, I thought you went back to Detroit to have you and Storm's baby. It is his, ain't it?" Jordan pushed her luck going for bad. "And dang you look good to be pregnant!"

Knowing Storm would be completely done when he saw the video, if he hadn't already, Kenya didn't feel the need to correct Jordan on her misinformed facts. It was obvious she hadn't actually been in the walk-in freezer; otherwise, she'd be running off at the mouth about that as well. For the time being, she'd let Jordan continue to breathe. At this point, Kenya had nothing else to lose, so one more dead body on her growing list wouldn't matter. It was nothing but God and time restrictions that saved Jordan's conniving life. Tossing her bag over her shoulder, Kenya briefly looked around once more then exhaled. Heading back to the lower level of the condo, she saw Brother Rasul standing at the end of the staircase nodding. Kenya knew he'd gotten London's body discreetly into the truck and was ready to leave.

"You good?" he asked.

"Yeah, I'm a hundred. We'll catch up with Storm later. Let's handle this other business first."

Shocked to see a naked female standing at the top of the stairs, he looked to Kenya who just shook her head guiding him out to the garage. "Let's just go. It ain't shit here for me anymore. This life is done." Kenya had him throw her bag in the back seat on the floor. A smile of satisfaction came across Brother Rasul's face, and Kenya's cell rang before they could get off the block.

STORM

Meanwhile, on the far side of town, Storm had gotten himself mentally together. After paying the funeral director the rest of the cash he owed him for his rush services, he went to see O.T. Literally sick to his stomach, he approached the casket. With both hands gripping the sides, his body started to shake uncontrollably. Closing his eyes, Storm wished he could just open them back up and all of the past few days would have been nothing more than a bad dream. His brother would be alive, talking that good shit he always did. Kenya would have been back at the house complaining about this and that. And he would be sneaking peeks at London's ever growing belly on the sly.

Unfortunately, when he did reopen his shut eyes, the horrible nightmare was still staring him in the face. All the dope money, bad bitches he'd fucked over the years, guns, property he owned, and expensive rides he possessed weren't gonna make this situation good. The tragic reality was what it was. "Damn, we should've gotten out this game a long damn time ago. I should've made the final call, but I didn't. This shit on me. A nigga dropped the fucking ball, bro." Storm repeatedly apologized to his brother's motionless corpse. "I fucked up! I'm sorry, bro!"

Wiping his eyes from the multitude of tears, Storm looked at all the flower arrangements that had come in. *Playas out here might've feared your ass, but them hoes always had love.* Storm read a few of the small attached cards to himself before moving over to the family guestbook. He wanted to see what mourners had beaten him there earlier that morning. *Oh, hell naw! What in the fuck?* He thought his red eyes must've been playing tricks on him. Kenya James's name was printed in black ink, bold as life directly on top of Anika's. *Kenya fucking James? This must be a fucking joke. Kenya? She's back? Naw, this must be a joke.* Wasting no time, Storm rushed out of the small chapel and into the director's office with the book in hand. Not caring that the man was on the phone, apparently consoling a potential customer, he started yelling. "Yo, yo." His voice got louder as he slammed the book on the desk. "I need to holler at you real quick; now!"

Sensing the drug dealer was not in the mood for common courtesy, he abruptly ended the call. "Yes, what's the problem? You don't like the job we've done? We did our absolute best."

"Naw, dawg, it ain't that." He pointed at the two names wrote in the book. "It's this right here."

"Okay, and?" The funeral director was at a loss.

"Kenya James's name is right damn here in this fucking book. What's it doing here? Why is it in here? I'm confused!"

"Calm down, sir. I guess she signed it earlier this morning. I'm sorry, you didn't inform me or the staff you wanted a closed viewing. I can adjust that immediately; no problem. Please forgive us."

"Hold up. What you saying? She was here? In this funeral home seeing my brother?"

"Yes, this morning. She, a man, and a tiny baby were here shortly after we opened. Like I said I didn't know you wanted a private viewing only. Allow me to make that clear to all the staff."

"Naw, hold up. A baby? A man? What man? What he look like? Was this her?" Storm reached in his back pocket pulling out his wallet then a picture of him and Kenya.

Nodding his head, the man confirmed that one of the young women who had been there this morning was indeed Kenya James. "The man she was with is from Detroit. He's a pretty big dude that's all I know." He had dealt with enough shadiness from drug dealers over the years to divulge as little information as possible. Saying he was Muslim, or the type of truck they were driving, would be on Storm to find out. After all, Brother Rasul had also paid him to do a job, so he wanted to stay out of any altercations that could possibly deviate from future business.

Leaving the book on the desk, Storm bolted out the door in utter disbelief. Darting into the parking lot, he jumped in his car, slamming the door shut. Dialing Kenya's number, he was shocked when she answered. "Yo, girl, damn. Where the hell you at? Where you been?"

"What? Don't worry where the fuck I'm at," she fired back at the top of her lungs. "Worry about the stankin' slut Jordan you got staying at my damn house, taking a shower in my fucking bathroom. That should be your new focus not where I'm at. Now bye, nigga. Beat it. Kick rocks."

"Hey wait, slow down, girl," Storm begged while pulling out into traffic. "My damn son!"

"Don't ask me nothing about his little shitty ass. You lucky I don't throw that ugly bastard of yours out the window. Now go fuck yourself, Storm, we done!"

Kenya hung up in his face. At first he thought it must have been a joke the funeral director was playing on him for some reason. Yet the fact she knew Jordan was at the condo proved it was true. She was back in town. Storm was overjoyed. His backbone was not far. *She probably still back at the house kicking Jordan's teeth in and dragging her by the hair.*

Running red light after red light, Storm finally made it to his block. *She didn't lie. London did have that baby! My son! My motherfucking son!* The thought of setting eyes on his baby was all he could think about. With O.T. gone, his first-born seed was all he had left to look forward to. Kenya might've been still on that "fuck you, nigga" bullshit and that was all right with him. Bitches come and go but, his son was his bloodline.

Chapter Twenty

JORDAN

What should have been a calm and normal morning was anything but that. All hell had broken loose, and in reality, the bona fide sack chaser had no one to blame except for herself. Having thrown on a track suit, Jordan snatched her cell off the floor. Her eyes were still burning as she tried to focus. Her skin still felt as if it were on fire. She was still trying to catch her breath and wrap her head around what had just taken place between her and Kenya. Nursing sore ribs alone with a busted lip, she held on to the banister making her way downstairs. *That bitch got me fucked up! She just lucky she caught me slipping, because if she didn't, I would have popped all the way off!* Somewhat disoriented from the ass whopping she'd just endured, Jordan struggled to see the cracked screen of her phone as it started to ring. *Now what? Who in the entire fuck is this about to be?* Caught in her feelings, she figured it had to be Storm demanding she get the hell out his house for fighting with Kenya. *At this point, I don't give two dry fucks if it is that nigga telling me to get the fuck on. He need to bring his ho ass back here and try to control that wild animal bitch he so in love with; put the cheating ho back on her leash.*

"Yeah, hello, what is it?" Ready to do verbal battle, her loud voice rudely rang throughout the house. "What? Say what?" she angrily responded to the caller. "Look y'all can pull the plug for all I care. Now please stop calling my damn shit. I got enough problems without worrying about my dingbat sister!"

After callously hanging up on the hospital she rubbed at her irritated eyes. Suddenly as if she needed any more surprises, Jordan smelled the pot she'd left simmering on the stove burning. Seconds later she almost jumped clean out of her skin. "What in the fuck else can happen today? I swear to God this ain't the time." As if on cue, the smoke detectors in the kitchen and rear pantry area starting ringing, causing Reckless to start back up barking. Turning the fire off underneath the pot, Jordan got yet another call. She was annoyed. Without attempting to look at the cracked screen, she sucked her teeth. Assuming it was the hospital again, she answered. "Damn, what part of don't call me again do you not comprehend? I thought I just said fuck that damaged bitch!"

"Hold up, trick. Who you think you talking to like that? You got me all the way twisted," Marco snarled ready to tear something up. "I swear, I'ma kill you about that smart mouth of yours! So yeah, okay, I just saw ol' girl and some big dude leave. Okay, nigga, so did she smack the fire out that ass for banging her man or what, you gutter side piece?"

Jordan knew by his informative statement, Marco must've been not too far away. She was terrified, but she knew as long as she was inside Storm's domain she'd be safe. "Nigga, didn't I say die in your sleep? So why you calling me? Kick rocks! Matter of fact, you coward, let me call Sprint right now!"

In between the dog's constant barking and the piercing sounds of the smoke detectors still going the noise level was too much to bear. Jordan had to do something to calm her shaky nerves. Taking a deep breath, she had no other choice. As she eased toward the other side of the kitchen, her heart raced. She would have to overcome her fear of the wild animal. Bravely walking toward the rear door, she unlocked it so some fresh air could circulate throughout the kitchen.

MARCO

Marco burped. Rubbing his stomach, he laughed at all the various items he had recently consumed. He'd spent the day and evening before cooking everything poor old Mrs. Farrow had in her refrigerator. And he'd snacked on everything in her cabinets. Having been on the run, the few measly meals he'd eaten at the hotel only put a small dent in his otherwise huge appetite. In between talking to the elderly woman's deceased body and eating he was in a weird zone. Strangely he propped her now rigor frame up in a chair to keep him company as he watched *Wheel of Fortune* and several reruns of *The Wire* on HBO. To pass the time away, Marco dialed Jordan's cell repeatedly. He was going ham, threatening the dancer with what he was intent on doing when he caught up to her. Although Jordan acted brave-hearted, he knew the goofy female was shook. *That chickenhead act like Storm can save her? Shit, that gay boy ain't gonna be able to save his own damn self! I'ma be on both they heads and anybody else's who gets in my damn way. Anyone who steps to me can get this work.*

Watching out the front picture window from the side, he could easily see the comings and goings at Storm's condo. After observing some random dude who apparently stayed there now leave, then Storm, Marco increased his "ho, I'm gonna body that ass" calls to Jordan. When she chose to answer, he went in, and when she didn't, he left bone-chilling messages until her mailbox was completely filled.

Minutes after she'd sworn to get her number changed, Marco saw a dark SUV slow down in front of the old woman's condo. *Damn, who in the fuck is this about to be?* Running to get his gun, he was soon relieved when it finally rode past his new Honeycomb Hideout. As he exhaled, he still stayed on guard as the vehicle turned into Storm's driveway. It took him all of five seconds to recognize a familiar face. "Oh, it's that crazy trick." He made reference to Kenya who'd just gotten out before her ride disappeared into the garage. "This about to be good as hell. Damn, I wish I was a fucking fly on the wall when she sees Jordan's bitch ass all up in her crib like she the queen bee! It's about to be some real-life horror movie bloodshed popping off inside that motherfucker."

Marco kept a careful eye out on the front door and the driveway and his ears wide open. He didn't want to potentially miss a thing. After a few minutes, he started to glance at the time on his cell phone and then back on the front door of the condo. He was posted. Even the crazy part of Omar getting killed by that little thug hopper couldn't steal his attention away from the window. Waiting for Jordan to be dragged out on the front lawn by her weave, fifteen or twenty minutes later, Marco was confused and speechless. The truck, which had parked inside the attached garage, pulled out and simply drove off. There was no big confrontation. There was no gunfire, no "bitch, who the fuck do you think you are," and no broken windows. The only thing Marco saw was just Kenya sitting in the passenger seat looking screw-faced pissed. Disappointed he didn't see hair ripped from Jordan's scalp or two sets of bare, exposed breasts flapping in the wind from torn shirts, he shrugged his shoulders.

Going into the kitchen to make yet another bowl of cereal and figure out his next move, Marco had to call Jordan in hopes of seeing if she'd gotten that ass smacked up or what. After a few rings, she picked up and cursed him out basically telling him what a rotten piece of shit she thought he was. With those insults along with being a coward, Marco couldn't hold his composure any longer. Throwing the bowl of Corn Flakes against the wall, he grabbed his gun. With contempt, he headed out the rear entrance of the elderly woman's condo. Once in the backyard, Marco was ready for war. As if he was some sort of an amateur contortionist, he somehow wedged his body through a hole in the fence connecting Mrs. Farrow's and Storm's properties. Thanks to Storm and his anger originally kicking the hole, Marco was easily creeping under the kitchen window. Listening to a dog barking and what sounded like smoke detectors, he peeped inside just in time to see Jordan head toward the door. Now would be payback time. Now he would teach her a deadly lesson about that "say anything to anybody" mouth of hers. *Ol' girl ain't tap that ass, but I'm that nigga; fo' sho.*

Thinking today must've been his lucky day, Marco grinned at the impending satisfaction. He knew in a matter of seconds he would be dancing in the devil's playground. One person on his long hit list would be getting what she had coming. Preparing himself to do whatever he needed to do, Marco took a deep breath. He leaned his body close against the rear wall of the condo as he saw Jordan push the steel gate open. As her arm was extending out, hand gripping the doorknob, he knew it was now or never. With one swift movement, the sworn killer yanked down on her wrist. Snatching her thick frame onto the concrete walkway, it was like Christmas, Easter, and his birthday all rolled into one.

"Oh my God, what the hell?" Jordan screamed out just before Marco's hand wrapped around her throat. Her eyes were already red and half shut from the bleach shower rinse Kenya had blessed her with; however, they popped wide open. Using all the strength she had left,

Jordan tried to fight back, but she quickly realized she had no win as Marco's grip tightened.

"What's up with you, bitch? What's good, hood rat?" Marco forced her back on to her feet. Laughing as if she were a joke, he fast walked her into the doorway knocking the side of her head against the frame. "I told you your ass couldn't hide from a nigga like me. See you used to dealing with them lames like Storm and his crew. Me, see, I ain't fake with my gangsta. I'm about that life for real."

"Wait. P . . . please," Jordan stuttered seeing the murderous rage in his eyes.

"Naw, girl, you wait. I wanna know what was that bullshit you was talking a few minutes ago, huh? You wasn't nothing but a waste of my sperm, a cum Dumpster."

The grasp he had on her boney throat was starting to cut off her air. Jordan soon felt her feet lift off the ground. Her feet started to kick as she fought to live. In the struggle, Marco's pistol fell to the ground. With the sounds of Jordan sobbing, Marco talking shit, and the gun hitting the marble floor Reckless continued to bark, even increasing his deep pitch.

"Urgg . . ." Her eyes rolled to the rear of her skull the more he applied pressure. She squirmed around while trying desperately to pry his hands from around her neck. She grew dizzy, and her lips started to tingle and feel numb. They were losing all of their color.

"You the first to go and when Storm get back to this motherfucker he gonna be the next. That's my word," he vowed with fury as he dragged her by the throat across the room. With no godly remorse, Marco slammed Jordan's head back and forth on the walk-in freezer door. With each jerk of her neck, he laughed. He wondered what Storm was gonna say when he came home and found him hidden behind his front door waiting to put a couple of hot ones up in him. *These busters gonna get*

enough of underestimating me! They only play at being
gangstas. That shit ain't learned; you born with it.

The black-hearted killer was tired of toying with his
once prey. With Jordan still fighting to live, Marco let go
of his strong neck grip. He then decided to bring an end
to his revenge where she was concerned. Vindictively,
he raised his foot kicking Jordan dead in the stomach
causing her to throw up at his feet. Repeating the dreadful action, she was about done as Reckless continued
to go crazy. Any other time, old Mrs. Farrow would be
probably ringing the doorbell complaining that there was
too much noise and commotion coming from Storm's
condo, but of course, that was not a factor.

Staggering from the brutal force of the last shoe sole
she felt an inch above her navel, Jordan flew into the
empty pantry door. In an effort to get away from Marco's
vicious attack, Jordan reached her arm up. Her T-shirt
somehow snagged on the doorknob turning it slightly
enough for it to open. Jordan, bruised and battered, then
fell back hitting her head on the marble flooring. She
was dizzy. She was out of breath. She was feeling herself
fighting to live. The kitchen seemed to be growing dark.
Seconds before losing consciousness, the always arrogant, self-serving, scheming female gasped in horror as
the huge, anxious-to-be-free albino pit busted out from
behind his in-house cage. Wanting nothing more than
to taste blood, the overweight beast pounced on Marco
knocking him into the wall.

"Oh, hell naw. What the fuck? Awww naw." Marco panicked not expecting the brutal attack. The self-proclaimed
thug hustler used both hands trying to pry the animal's
sharp teeth from his upper shoulder blade just as Jordan
had attempted to do to his. "Oh, shit! Fuck! Fuck Damn!
Naw!" Aggressively he fought the four-legged creature
the best he possibly could. Yet as the seconds seemed to
drag by the grueling assault never let up.

Reckless was in rare "attack, crush, kill, destroy" mode. He was trained to go and was doing just that. The animal that hadn't been fed since the evening before happily enjoyed the taste of human flesh. Every movement Marco made, the pit bull counteracted by increasing his iron mouth grip. Digging deeper into his victim's skin, Reckless's teeth ripped away at chunks of the human's neck making his way down his body.

Panicked and almost out of breath, Marco widened his eyes, desperately searching for his gun. They darted from one side of the floor to the next. He finally made eye contact. Unfortunately, his trusty weapon was yards away. Making an attempt to get in that direction, he felt Reckless temporarily loosen his massive jaw hold from his bloodied shoulder. Marco knew it was now or never if he wanted to survive. He had to make his move, and he did. Crawling on the floor, he went over Jordan's motionless body.

In a matter of mere seconds, Reckless showed Marco the same amount of compassion as he had shown Jordan: none. He was doomed. Marco collapsed from the weight of the dog attacking him from behind. Tearing away at his jugular vein with razor-sharp paws, Reckless seemed to be in heaven. Marco wanted to yell out to the dog to suck his dick, but he couldn't; his vocal cords were severed. In the midst of the one-sided battle, it soon became apparent that Storm would no longer have to be concerned with Marco and his revenge-filled threats. Out of all the men, women, and even kids Marco Meriwether had brutally murdered, beaten, raped, disrespected, harassed, taken advantage of, and had no overall regard for, finally it took a wild, untamed animal such as himself to bring an end to his reign of terror.

Chapter Twenty-one

POLICE

"Okay, everyone suit up and get prepared. With all the information Sergeant Kendricks has provided us with over the past few days he learned from Paris, it's a definite go. The prosecutor's office rep will be here momentarily with the signed warrants. And then Tony Christian aka Storm will be regretting the day he was born. We finally have enough evidence to lock him up for the rest of his natural life." Detective Malloy was trying to contain his glee. With a brave confidence, he put his own bulletproof vest on just a couple of blocks away from Storm's condo. Incidentally, it was also the location of the recovered stolen minivan that had been discovered with Marco Meriwether's fingerprints inside.

With anticipation of finally closing several major cases that had been dead ends up until now, Malloy checked his revolver. Seeing it was fully loaded and ready for action he then proceeded to check his riot pump as well. This was the day he and most of the entire department had been waiting for. The day Storm, always eluding getting caught back up in the system, would be put in handcuffs. It didn't matter his suspended partner Sergeant Kendricks had conned the damning information from Paris. It didn't matter that she was deemed mentally unstable. All of that was beyond the point. The hard, cold fact still remained that Storm was going down, dead or

alive this go-around. And as far as Detective Malloy was
concerned the choice would be his.

STORM

"Look, Kenya, I want to see my damn baby. Nothing
more nothing less. What part of that don't you understand?"

"So damn what? 'I wanna see my damn baby,'" she
spitefully mocked after reading him the riot act about
Jordan being back at the condo. "People in hell straight
want ice water, but oh, well. You know how that bullshit
go."

"Yo, I'm serious as fuck. I'm not playing around with
you no more. If you still care anything about a nigga, at
least you'll let me see my kid. I mean, damn. I know you
bitter as fuck behind everything that jumped off."

"Bitter? Me? Now, why would you think I was bitter?
Because you got me all out here in these streets looking
stupid as hell while you banging every ho at the club?
Or bitter because you had the nerve to get my own sister
knocked up in the house I lay my head down at night?
Which one, nigga? Please tell me."

"Look, you silly-ass little bitch," he fired back tired
of all the cat-and-mouse insult games she was playing.
"Right about now I'm working on a short fuse and trust
me when I tell you this ain't the time to try to be all tough.
Now like I done said a million times before, I ain't fucked
none of them dancers at the club, and now all I wanna
do is see my baby, my seed. Where the hell is London
at anyhow? Do she know about you doing all this shit to
block me from seeing our baby?"

"Damn, all right now. I heard that. You said 'our baby'
prouder than a motherfucker. That's all you give a hot
shit about with your shady, slimeball, backstabbing ass:
that baby and my sister." Kenya hung up the phone but
answered it when Storm called right back

"Yeah, whatever, with your jealous, insecure ass. And like I just said before you hung up, where is London at anyhow? She letting you play games with the baby like you doing?"

"Fuck your baby momma London, fuck you, and double fuck y'all bastard-ass baby," she hissed with intense fury. "Y'all can all three be a family in hellfire for all I care. I'm good doin' me."

"Please, Kenya! Why you doing this bullshit? I always had your back and you doing me like this? I done dogged out motherfuckers and bitches who been crazy loyal to me over the years just because you didn't like them. I had them to get the fuck on instantly just on the strength of your word and you bugging. You questioning my loyalty to you." Storm managed to beg to see his son in between Kenya still cursing him out for Jordan being at the house and hanging up on him again. Of course, he called back.

"Okay, bitch, I'm done fucking around with your dumb ass. You had a nigga all in for you, jumping through hoops to be down for you, loyal to you. And now you a straight-up bug."

"Yup, I showl in the hell is," she hissed not trying to hear or accept anything he was saying. "I see you was so damn loyal you got a baby by my sister and one of your hoes lying up in my house washing her stank ass in my shower. Boy, bye."

Storm had been keeping his eye on the road the entire time he had been arguing with who he thought was the love of his life. Having lived with Kenya all this time, he knew she was prone to go through one of her many emotional tantrums. He prayed this was just another and she would calm down and come home. Quickly he swerved the car up in front of his condo behind Jordan's. *Damn, why I even let this dumb ho come and crash here? I knew that shit was gonna blow up in my face. Fuck!*

Storm's tires screeched as he slammed down on the brakes. Paying careful attention to each and every vehicle on the block, sadly he didn't see any signs of Kenya. His heart sank. He also didn't take notice of the man the funeral director described who he had assumed must've been Brother Rasul. He started to get a strange feeling in the pit of his stomach. Noticing the garage was wide open, Storm knew that at least Kenya had actually been there since no one else but him, O.T., and she had the security code. *I hope this fool is just inside posted on the couch with London and my baby. Maybe they both got Jordan ass hemmed up in a closet scared to come out. Damn, this been the worst few months in my life. All a nigga wanted to do is live right. Take care of my girl and my seed and get money. Damn!*

Anxious to see if Kenya was possibly still inside with his newborn, Storm turned off the engine. Desperate in his intentions, he jumped out of the car. Before the visibly distraught thug could walk across the grass, he was startled. A woman suddenly appeared from behind one of the bushes. "Damn, where you come from?" Storm paused while still keeping his eyes focused on the front door of his condo.

"Hey, now; what up, doe." Anika smiled showing damn near every tooth in her mouth. "What's going on, dude? How you been?"

Storm was thrown off by her presence; however, he did see her name on O.T.'s guestbook back at the funeral home. "Well, you know this past week ain't been the best for a nigga, ya feel me? I mean all things considered." He lowered his head before looking back up in her eyes. "I saw you stopped by to pay your respects to my brother. Seriously, no bullshit, I appreciate that for real."

"Let's keep it a hundred. It ain't nothing; ain't no thang." Anika smiled seductively running her hands through her long braids. "I told you in the car we was family now didn't I? And real family do real shit."

"Yeah, we good, but still I wanna say good looking. Plus I saw the flowers 'the family' sent. That shit really say something to me, you feel me? Hit home."

"Ain't shit like a family's love, and that's straight up." Anika's voice purred as she spoke rubbing her hand seductively on Storm's shoulder.

"Yeah, Anika, you right. A family's love," he repeated thinking about seeing his newborn son for the first time. That was all that mattered to him: finally laying eyes on his baby boy. He had dreamed about that moment for what seemed like a lifetime. Now shortly his dream would be coming true. Snatching him back into reality and the here and now, his cell vibrated indicating he had a text message. Glancing down, he saw it was from Kenya. Pushing the button, he downloaded the two attachments that were envelopes posted in the upper right corner of his screen. Before he could see what was what, he heard a loud, thundering sound. That ear-shattering noise was swiftly followed by a strong force knocking him off his feet. Storm's body was lifted up and dropped down onto the grass. As he lay there dazed, he had no idea what had just taken place. The street-born hooligan was oblivious he'd just been shot. With his cell still clutched in his trembling hand, Storm's eyes barely opened to see the now fully downloaded picture of a small newborn baby: his baby.

Anika was menacing as she stood towering over him. With sarcastic satisfaction, she smirked with smoking gun still in hand. "See boo-boo, I told you we were a hundred percent family. And family deals with family business, you feel me? So it's better you learned this painful lesson early on in dealing with your newfound family. You know, before anyone else has to pay for your fuckups and short-ass payments!" Glancing upward, Anika saw several police cars, lights flashing. Directly on the cars' tails was what appeared to be a raid van barreling down the usually quiet block. "Damn, Storm, what a waste. You had major potential; we all saw the shit in you. It was like you was born to do this street shit, kinda kingpin status. But, hey, right about now it's the point and principle. Like Daddy said, no fucking shorts!"

Storm paid what he could on the enormous ticket owed. Yet unfortunately, it wasn't enough. If Kenya, being self-ish and unreasonable, hadn't stolen his stash money, he would've had enough. But now she was ghost, and she was going to be coming up off his money and jew-elry. She was still going to be out here among the living, walking the streets doing what dirty bitches like her did. Storm was bitter with dealing with his sudden coldblooded triple dose of reality but had no more time to focus on her. He was lying face down on the grass, chok-ing on his own blood, incidentally in the same spot O.T. had been dropped at by his surprise assailant. "Please, my son," Storm somehow managed to mutter as a portion of the rear half of his head was blown off. "My baby boy. Kenya, why . . . I love . . ."

Knowing she was sent to do a job, Anika was not moved one bit by his plea of scrambled words. A true street solder for the family she was loyal to, she eagerly raised her handgun once more intent on ending Storm's life and any chance he'd ever have of holding his son. "Sorry I couldn't have gotten none of that big-ass dick you packing, but it's all in the game. Family is everything and family always comes first. Easy come, easy the fuck go." With a matter of seconds, her finger once more tightened around the trigger. Pulling back, she let three more quick rounds off all finding their mark: the upper chest area. It was done. It was over. It was definitely over.

Tony Storm Christian, a staple in the drug dealer game he loved so much, was gone. He was no more, like O.T. The once bright sun had set on the brother's reign. Anika had come to do what she was sent to do. Her murderous mission was completed. Still on point, she wanted to try to make her way to her car, which was parked one block over. However, Malloy and his team had other plans for the femme fatale.

"Freeze," he loudly ordered upon seeing Storm lying near her feet not moving. "Drop that goddamn gun! Drop it! I'm warning you! Don't make this ugly!"

"It already is, playboy; it already is." Anika devilishly smirked still standing tall. True to her own words, family takes care of family. She raised her pistol sucking on the barrel of the gun like it was a rock-hard dick waiting to get topped off.

"Don't do it," Malloy urged as huge beads of perspiration started to form on his worried brow. Locking eyes with the blond-braided beauty, he yelled out once more as she pulled the trigger splattering her own brains on the nearby bushes.

Malloy was left speechless. He was infuriated to say the least, angry at the world. As they covered Storm's lifeless body with a beige tarp, the longtime officer held on to the signed arrest warrants, which were now worthless. He couldn't believe his luck. At this point, there was nothing left to do but at least execute the search warrants for the address Storm called home. Ramming down the condo doors, the fugitive apprehension team was met by an irate, still-blood-thirsty Reckless who had to be put down immediately; the shot killed him instantly. With a quick search of the premises, soon they discovered Marco Meriwether's deceased dog-mauled body. It was stretched out alongside stripper Jordan Jamison, whose prints were also found inside the hotel room where Big Doc B was found murdered.

"Well, at least we can charge her with the doctor's homicide." Detective Malloy expressed a small amount of satisfaction knowing she was a small fish to fry in compassion to Storm and his organization.

As the neighbors again came out from behind the once tranquil confines of their homes, one of their own was noticeably absent. They each covered their mouths and turned their heads in disbelief when old Mrs. Farrow's body was discovered after retracing Marco's steps. A few of them used to gossip behind Kenya's back when she first magically appeared to start living with Storm. They felt the Detroit-born female would bring trouble to their gated and otherwise picture perfect community and, considering the events that had popped off in the months since she arrived, they were correct.

Chapter Twenty-two

KENYA

As the four of them turned into the funeral home parking lot, things seemed to be surreal to Kenya. Brother Rasul got out of the vehicle going inside. His mission was clear. He had to inform the director he had London's body in the rear of his truck wrapped in a rug. The Islamic man of faith wanted him to know that all was a total go on their end and they could proceed with their illegal plans to ship the deceased back to Detroit so she could have a proper burial. As he disappeared behind the double doors to put the plan into full throttle, Kenya sat in the truck in a semi-daze.

I don't need that cheating, backstabbing motherfucker! *First he was knocking off my rotten-ass, no-good sister like I wasn't there every night sucking his dick, but now Jordan? Now that slimeball got that nothing ass lying up in my crib, washing her stanking ass in my shower! Damn, I was a fool for that faggot! I hate the fuck outta him! On everything I used to love, I swear I should take this baby he care so much about and choke the little bastard out. I got a right mind to throw his crybaby ass right in that Dumpster over there!* Still distraught from finding Jordan in the house she'd decorated, taking a shower and cooking like she was the new queen of the trap, Kenya sat back in the passenger seat. Squirming in the passenger seat, she grew more and more infuriated.

As her cell kept ringing, her fury at and animosity for Storm increased. *Fuck his fake ass. Now he wanna be begging me. Fuck him!* Hanging up on the once love of her life repeatedly, she finally let him get out how he wanted to see his son so damn bad and how Jordan ain't mean shit to him. *And this off-brand nigga had the nerve to say he loved me in the same breath as asking where my sister was at. I hate his cheating ass! One day somebody gonna fuck his lying ass up! Karma is a real bitch and one day soon he gonna meet that bad bitch for how done treated me!*

Kenya's cruel thoughts were abruptly interrupted as she heard Li'l Stone start to cry from the back seat. His tiny cries were giving her chills. It was as if someone or something were nudging her shoulder to come to his innocent aid. Kenya was hardcore as they came. She fought the feeling and put up a good fight, but she soon lost the battle. Being a woman first before a bitch, her maternal instinct kicked in. She wanted to give her tiny, helpless nephew a bottle or his pacifier. She stared back over her shoulder and paused. If she chose to put the infant out of his misery and herself for having to hear his pleas, she'd be too close to his mother, her sister, who was only a few feet away still frozen, undoubtedly stiff as a board.

Thinking about London and reminiscing about her grandmother, who were both now gone, a part of Kenya got a small bit of remorse. Fighting a guilty conscience for all the bullshit her jealous behavior had caused, she got herself back together. After getting her emotions in check, she got out of the truck. Standing in the semi-empty funeral home parking lot, she stretched her arms while taking a deep breath. She wished she were back at home, in Detroit, sitting on the stairs of her childhood home. Kenya wanted nothing more than to turn back the hands of time, but regretfully she knew that task wasn't possible. London was dead by her hands, and she wasn't coming back. That was her reality, one she'd have to live with the rest of her life.

Opening the rear door of the vehicle, Kenya took her cell out taking a few more pictures of the fussing infant. As her finger trembled, she sent them to Storm. Even though she felt he needed to suffer a little bit more before she'd possibly let him off the hook, she did it anyway. In her twisted mind, since London was gone, maybe they'd have a slim chance to make shit right. That was, if he was willing to practically kiss her ass.

Closing her eyes, she reopened them seeing her twin sister was still in the rear hatch wrapped in the rug. Suddenly she felt a strange chill come over her body.

"Damn, excuse me."

Kenya was startled as she turned around seeing an older woman standing practically face to face with her. "Do you need something, miss? Is there something I can help you with?"

"Yes, there is." The lady struggled to speak as she frowned with a strong flow of tears streaming down her jaws.

Putting both hands on her hips, Kenya was confused but sympathetic. It didn't take her long to now recognize the woman as the same lady she'd bumped into earlier inside of the funeral home. "Are you all right? You need me to call somebody out here for you or what? You seem like you need some help or something."

"No, I don't think anyone can help me but you. Matter of fact I know you are the only one who can." The woman paused. She was obviously in her emotions as her face appeared distraught.

"Huh? What, me?" Kenya questioned wondering what the strange older woman could possibly be talking about.

"Look, lady, I don't mean no type of disrespect, but I don't even know you. So if you want me to go get somebody outta the funeral home, I can."

"What, are you serious right now? We've apparently been sharing all this time, and you don't even know me? Is that how you young girls carry yourselves these days, so nonchalant about the things you do and the people you hurt along the way?"

Kenya had enough problems to deal with and some random off-the-wall-talking, crying-ass lady was not gonna be one of them. Kenya wanted to get her away from the side of truck before she noticed her sister's dead body and made more of a scene than she already was doing. "Sharing, me and you? Look here, lady, I already done told you I don't know you from a hole in the wall so I'ma need for you to get the fuck away from me okay? I'm straight on whatever game you trying to run. I ain't got the time or the patience okay? So just beat it before I start really disrespecting my elders."

"Game. Me running game." The hysterical woman stepped closer to Kenya with one hand extended fully outward. "Just tell me, why? Why in God's name did you do it? Why? Why did you think it was okay?"

Placing one hand up to shield the brightly beaming sunlight, Kenya raised her eyebrow. She couldn't believe it. Her heart sank to her feet. Ashamed and embarrassed, Kenya took a good look at what the woman was holding. "Oh my God," she whispered underneath her breath while watching the video of her sucking Big Doc B's dick. "Where did you—"

"Don't worry about that, you lowlife, home-wrecking tramp. Just know he was my husband. He was the love of my life and the father of my kids, and because of you and your slutty lifestyle, he's gone. So just tell me, why?

Why do I have to explain to my children that Daddy is gone and never coming home? Why do you think it's okay for you to be out here in the world among the living and he's gone? It's not fair. You smiling and coming to see someone in this place when you the one who should be in a casket."

At a loss of words or an explanation for the XXX video, Kenya momentarily lowered her head in shame. As the woman continued her verbal tirade, the Detroit-born, self-proclaimed diva had lost her nerve to face the facts of what she had done and who she had become. As bad as she didn't want to admit it, the scorned wife was indeed 100 percent correct. She had done way too much over the prior year to even be standing here to see the awful illicit video. Kenya quickly had flashbacks to the many lives she had ruined. She got chills knowing that she had caused so much chaos and destruction to others. She knew her grandmother would be disappointed that despite all her efforts to provide her and London with love and support after their mother's murder, she had turned out to be who she was. Kenya took ownership that she was no more than a true menace to herself, her family legacy, and any other person she came in contact with.

Suddenly the sun seemed to beat down on her even more. Her head was pounding. The sides of her temples seemed to be keeping a rhythmic pace with her racing heart. She couldn't face Doc's wife any longer. Kenya hastily turned back around to get Li'l Stone out of his car seat and go inside with Brother Rasul. She felt it was best to just remove herself from the explosive confrontation until Doc's distraught wife left.

Leaning over in the truck trying to block out the angry woman's screams of betrayal, Kenya was caught off guard. She definitely wasn't ready when the half-crazed woman attacked. Kenya unexpectedly felt the lady grab her from behind. Feeling the woman's hot breath on her neck was swiftly followed by a sharp pain. Not being able to break free because of the position she was in, Kenya reached upward wrapping both hands around her own neck. She was confused. She was in immediate denial. But the damage was done. It was too late. Doc's wife had used one of her husband's many surgical scalpels to slit her throat.

Kenya's world was spinning. Her eyes were bulging out of her head. They blinked repeatedly as if they were trying to focus. She couldn't speak. She could not scream out for help or even breathe. Her once perfect world had spun out of control. Kenya's drama-filled life was flashing before her eyes as her attacker walked away in a zombie-like trance with the bloody death weapon still dripping from her blood.

Being top dog in high school, the day Gran died, and the first day she danced at Head's Up, meeting Storm, Swift getting killed in her hallway, finding Deacon's head in the fish tank, her having to shoot Chocolate Bunny and, most memorable, the day she found out her twin sister was pregnant by her man; all those memories, some good and some most certainly bad, took over her thoughts. Life was short, as Gran used to always say. And now as Kenya lay slumped over on Li'l Stone bleeding out on his powder blue sleeper, she realized that fact, but it was much too late. All the manipulation, plotting, and scheming had run its course. It was over for the Detroit-born boss bitch, and she was paying the ultimate price: death. No more "I'm sorry," no more "I can make shit right," and no more "maybe things can get better." For Kenya James, just like her twin, London who was wrapped in a rug on the other side of the truck seat, it was lights out. They would both soon be back with their parents in heaven or hell. Ashes to ashes, dust to dust.

Epilogue

Six Months Later

Convicted on first-degree murder charges, Jordan sat behind bars on death row wondering how things had gotten so fucked up. Her plans of being a boss's bitch and taking over Kenya's place were over with. Considering everyone she dealt with were criminals, dead, or just didn't give a shit about her conniving ass, she failed to produce a witness who was willing to testify on her behalf to exactly where she was when Big Doc B was killed. Her fingerprints were all over the room and, unfortunately, the surveillance tape failed to show the time she left the hotel premises. She was cooked and knew it. She had offered to tell them a boatload of other crimes and awful transgressions that she knew of, but none of her confessions really mattered. There was no one to prosecute. Her snitching would be in vain.

Since Marco was dead, someone had to pay. The public was infuriated about all the surge of murders that had taken place over the past year. It was more than just the residents of the city, but the nation as well. They wanted at least one high-profile arrest and conviction, so Detective Malloy gave them one: Jordan's ass served on a silver platter. Since her sister had recovered from Marco's brutal attack, she not once had been to visit Jordan in prison. Maybe at Jordan's execution she'd show up, just maybe, but only time would tell.

Paris finally came back to her right mind. She was doing well physically only to lose her mental state of mind once again after finding out the supposed patient who'd pretended to care so much about her was the police and was only using her for information. Pretending to accept his apology, she played it cool like most predators did when hunting their prey. When she got the opportunity, Paris grabbed his firearm. He didn't see it coming. The staff didn't see it coming and, truth be told, Paris didn't know what she was going to do to get revenge on him until she did it. Wasting no time, she raised her arm and discharged the police-issued firearm. Two rounds were fired causing loud thunderous sounds to ring out and echo off the hospital walls. As if she were a trained marksman, each bullet found a home: one in the temple for his betrayal and the other directly through the heart. As she was already mentally disabled and under strict psychiatric care and monitoring, no criminal charges could be pressed. She would literally get away with murder. Spending her days and nights in the nuthouse, Paris had no idea whatsoever that her new roommate, Big Doc B's widow, had killed her best friend. Maybe one day in group therapy the truth would come out, but for now, it was what it was.

Back in Detroit, Brother Rasul was fighting with his own demons. Stunned at the strange turn of events, he was still dealing with the fact he was forced to ship both Kenya, whom he'd fallen in love with, and London's bodies home to be buried next to their parents, grandmother, and uncle. Finding Kenya bleeding to death in the rear of his truck was almost more than he could stand. As he held her in his arms begging for Allah to spare her life, Kenya slipped away. Always a strong man, physically and mentally, he felt broken. There was nothing he could do to change the consequences his friend had endured. He knew he should have followed what Kenya wanted to do and stay back in Detroit, but he had to force the issue and her hand. Overcome with his faith, he did what he felt was best. Not only for him, but who he would soon find out was an orphaned Li'l Stone as well. After receiving the devastating news that Storm had been murdered at the hands of "the family," Brother Rasul wanted to man up. It was in his nature to do so. A man of convictions, he knew the baby deserved a chance at having a normal life and childhood.

Wanting to be a part of something that was good and pure he changed his life and how he moved. Trying his best to hide his devastation over Kenya's untimely demise, he and Fatima patched up their differences. After a short time of him proving to her that she was his true soul mate they got married so that they could give their newly adopted son, Kalif, aka Li'l Stone, a proper upbringing. He paid an enormous fee to have documents falsified to make them his legal parents. Eerily, each and every day the small baby grew, Brother Rasul could see something cold in the boy's eyes. It was something that sent chills down his spine.

Fatima was nurturing as any mother could be to a child, but the boy was having none of it. Even though Kalif was only six months old, it seemed like he'd been here before. Ironically, he was the spitting image of Storm down to the way his nose was shaped and the expression he had when pissed. There was some sort of sinister glare in his eyes when he would drink his bottle or get his diaper changed. Even his shit smelled like trouble. The couple prayed five times a day and twice nightly he'd grow up to be nothing like his drug-dealing father who would get paid by any means needed to pop off. But unfortunately, they knew this infant's gangster-minded bloodline ran deep. Brother Rasul, Fatima and, strange as it may seem, even little Kalif knew he was destined to one day grow up to be a kingpin of Detroit.

Only time would tell.

The End